WORLD
SHAPER

WORLD SHAPER

THEODORE KRULIK

WORLD SHAPER

iUniverse books may be ordered through booksellers or by contacting:

iUniverse
1663 Liberty Drive
Bloomington, IN 47403
www.iuniverse.com
1-800-Authors (1-800-288-4677)

ISBN: 978-1-5320-7073-0 (sc)
ISBN: 978-1-5320-7075-4 (hc)
ISBN: 978-1-5320-7074-7 (e)

Library of Congress Control Number: 2019902768

Print information available on the last page.

iUniverse rev. date: 03/12/2019

To the love of my life,
Forever friend,
Companion in all things,
My inspiration,
Roberta

ACKNOWLEDGEMENTS

I thank all the members, past and present, of the creative writing class of the Si Beagle Learning Center in Queens, New York of the United Federation of Teachers. Among these first readers, I must single out the following: Terry Riccardi, superb editor who often pointed out technical errors in my writing that I would have otherwise missed and whose suggestions improved the work at hand; Jim Cunningham, our creative writing teacher, whose kindness and encouragement enabled me to produce at my best; and Allan Yashin, playwright and humorist, who actively engaged in field work so that I could depict an accurate picture of Greenwich Village.

I also thank Steven Adler for his expert information on police procedure in the NYPD and the protocols for a police arrest; and Dr. Saul Sokolow for explaining the diagnosis and treatment of brain trauma and concussions

My thanks also to my dear friends, Bernice and John Lange for their continued interest in my progress on this novel. Their genuine enthusiasm bolstered me even in the toughest times.

WORLD SHAPER

CHAPTER ONE
Targeted

I was being watched. I'd been watched for years. He hadn't done anything to me and I'd never actually spotted him following me. But it was the same person whenever I caught him at it.

How did I know?

Because I recognized what he was seeing. Me. Oh, not as I am now at twenty-eight years old. No. Most often, what he envisioned was myself as a teenager with longish brown hair falling over my forehead.

Always that vision in his head. Some time ago, I figured out why. Whenever he decided he was close enough, he deliberately thought of that image of me. Only one reason why he'd do that.

He knew I could read his mind.

Last week, I spotted him for the first time. I saw his face, one very much like someone I saw an age ago. We had a confrontation of sorts. I'll know him for sure next time.

It was broad daylight. About three in the afternoon. Two-story buildings on either side of the street. Bright sunshine and a bitterly cold wind made me squint and pull up the collar of my woolen coat. I was bent forward fighting the chill breeze when two teen-age boys, about seventeen or eighteen, ran playfully toward me. They were laughing as the frosted air pushed them along.

The shorter teen, black hair, dark eyes, his lips twisted into a smirk, had me in his thoughts. He saw me as an older guy with veins running along the sides of my neck and up through my cheeks and eyes.

That's not me! I thought. *My veins don't stick out like that!*

"Hi," he said once he got close. About my height, he stared me down at eye level. He raised his arm to keep me from walking away. "Got any bread to spare?" I felt his quickening heart, his eagerness to do something. He viewed me as weak and stupid and helpless. I saw those sensibilities in his mind.

The second boy, taller by two inches, with short hair the color of chalk dust and similarly-colored fuzz on his cheeks and chin, spit out in a short burst: "Hamburgers." He pointed with a dirty finger, tapping me in the chest. "And fries." His neck and head jutted forward with each word. "For both of us. Hungry. Got no money."

I couldn't read the taller boy, let's call him Sand Hair, at all. From the shorter boy, Dark Eyes, I sensed instant hatred. Maybe because I wore eyeglasses, expensive Italian-made steel frames. They enhanced my cheek bones.

Dark Eyes pounded my face as I lay sprawled on the sidewalk, smashing my glasses, kicking me in the groin, grinning at my pain. He didn't like me at all.

"Got nothin' to say?" said Dark Eyes. He turned to Sand Hair. "I don' think he wants to talk to us."

"How come?" Sand Hair looked from his pal to me. He was the more dangerous one, I realized. With no image in his head for me to pick up, I read: KILL THE TOAD! Not words exactly. Attitude and inchoate sounds, like the passing of a fire truck siren in a tornado.

Sand Hair pressed his hand into my shoulder, pushing into the fabric of my heavy coat with his dirty fingers. "Don't you want to help us? We just want something to eat. Can't you help us out?"

I tried a step back but he held his grip on my coat. I decided on using my well-known charm, edged by a bit of humor. "Sorry, fellas. Cold out. Gotta get home."

"I hear you," said Dark Eyes. "Got you a nice big home, do you? Maybe a wife? Or a girlfriend?"

"Food?" said Sand Hair. "We're real hungry, you know?"

"Maybe spend some time with your girlfriend, too? Get to know her real good? You gots to have a little tail at home."

Immediately, I got the picture. Literally. Dark Eyes imagined an attractive Everywoman with auburn hair and Italian-framed eyeglasses, wearing nothing else, tied to a bed at the four corners. I blinked several times to get rid of the hot steel rod he was using on her. Eyes shut for maybe five seconds, I finally eradicated the image.

An icy drop of perspiration under my coat, under my shirt, under my V-neck slid down the center of my back. It left me shivering.

I reached into my pocket for something to use. Keys, maybe. For a second I thought I might use them for brass knuckles. But these two sociopaths-in-training had it all over me in terms of physical daring and strength. I couldn't take them. No way.

But I knew something that they didn't. This was my neighborhood. I was a few short blocks from home. Middle of the week; three-thirty in the afternoon. Late October.

Someone I knew would be walking by any moment now. I looked at the sidewalks, front and across the street. Empty for the moment. Someone was bound to walk by. Any of my friendly neighbors. That would break up this little party. Watch it, you psychos!

Any time now. Okay, there. Old Mrs. What's-her-name with her cane, crossing the street to the other side. I'll just call out . . . what WAS her name?

Get ready to run, you bastards! Someone will show up. Any time now.

Any time now.

Any time now.

The boys circled around me, Dark Eyes right up to my face. "Say sumpthin,' Dimsucks. You look like you wanna say sumpthin.'"

He was reaching into his own pants pocket. I couldn't read him at all then. Perhaps I shut off his imaginings completely after blinking out his thoughts of the girl. He grinned when he grasped something in his pocket. I didn't think he was going to pull out his keys.

Pre-teen Alex in my face, smiling shyly, brushing back a clump of brown hair from his forehead.

The image lasted maybe five seconds. Then I stood facing Sand Hair. A heavy shadow seemed to step out from behind the tall boy.

It was a large man, muscular build, in a gray coat. "What's going on here?" Loud. Deep. Strong.

The shorter teen turned to the new presence behind his pal. Dark Eyes lifted something in his hand. It was mostly hidden from me. I hoped it wasn't a gun.

The large man was about an inch taller than Sand Hair but he looked the more dangerous of the two. He grabbed Sand Hair by the back of the neck, lifted him and tossed him into the street. Sand Hair screamed as he flew into the air and landed on his stomach. A car hit the brakes an inch before the sprawled teenager. Sand Hair jerked up, stared at the stranger in amazement, and sprinted down the street, a wagon train of cars squealing to a stop and beeping their horns.

The man, meaty unsmiling face, dark eyes far apart, large build, faced the remaining kid. He stared at Dark Eyes who still had some small black thing in the hand of his crooked arm.

"What are you going to do with that?' said the man.

The boy's dark eyes grew dull. He slipped the thing back in his pocket, backed slowly away, turned, and ran along the sidewalk in the direction opposite his friend.

I watched him race to the corner, go right, and disappear. I turned back to the stranger and he was gone. I couldn't believe it! He couldn't have run *that* fast. We were in the middle of the block with no obvious hiding places. He was simply gone.

Like he never existed.

CHAPTER TWO
Mr. Quiver

My old friend gazed at me from across his desk. He was assessing me, his mind full of curiosity. "How come you decided to look me up now?"

Why? I wondered that myself. "There's so much I have to explain. We haven't seen each other in so many years. I had some of this ability when we were teenagers that summer in Monticello. Even before that incident in my parents' store. You see, I nearly died once and actually died two times in my life and returned. When I revived each time, I had something more added to my special gift."

"What gift?"

"Well, I've gone this far. Here goes: I have to look at a person, usually someone I know. Or someone who is expressing strong emotions. I need to be familiar with a person before I begin picking up what is on his mind."

"Like you are now, Alex? With me?"

"That's right. Like I am now. With you. I see my own face in your eyes. As I am. Yet you see a face with eyes that are too sharp. You see me with doubt, with a sense that I'm to be feared. You don't trust me."

"You picked up on all that?"

"Yes. My gift goes further. You see me grabbing you by the shirt. You're pushing me away."

"How can you know that? How can you know what's --? Oh."

"That's it. You've got it now. I pick up what you're feeling. And what you imagine might happen. I see your perception of things. That's the gift I have."

"I've heard of people who have had near-death experiences. That sometimes, if their brain had been damaged, they get enhanced senses. A blind man gains extraordinary hearing. A brain-damaged person becomes a savant with a remarkable skill, like the ability to add numbers instantly."

"Yes. That's right."

"So, what is it you want from me?"

"I need your trust. I need your help. Last week I saw that stranger with the wide-apart eyes. The man I believe has been watching me for years. We . . . interacted."

My friend leaned forward, his eyes intense. "Go on."

I proceeded to tell him about the two teenagers, Dark Eyes and Sand Hair. And my encounter with the big man.

"Now this man with the far apart eyes has made himself known to me. I need to know why. What does he want from me? Then, also, I've gotten something. Something tangible."

My friend, eyes staring, asked, "What was that?"

"I got something yesterday. A note slipped under my door. I found it when I woke up in the morning.

"I sensed nothing as I picked it up but reading it left me nervous as hell." I pulled a folded sheet of paper inside a plastic baggie from my jacket. I unfolded the plastic and held it out for my friend. "Here it is."

Alex

I know you are special. I've known for a long time. I don't intend hurting you. But I will be around to help again when you need it.

Someday I may let you know why I'm interested. Patience, young man.

Best,
Mr. Quiver

My friend grinned as he looked from the note to me. I recognized some of the silliness I had seen in him from that long ago time we spent together.

"Mr. Quiver?" he said. "A tad melodramatic. I guess he knows you're a famous writer now, huh? Poking fun at the weird stuff you write by calling himself 'Mr. Quiver.'"

I smiled back. "Seems to have a sense of humor, doesn't he? Don't know why he picked that name. Doesn't mean anything to me. But I didn't see anything frivolous or melodramatic when he rescued me from those teenagers."

"Okay. I understand. Sort of. What do you want me to do?"

"Keep the note. Maybe it will help. It's in this plastic bag so you can check for fingerprints. If he actually left any."

"I'd like to know a bit more first. About you. About how you became so special. How did it happen initially?"

"Okay," I said, and took a deep breath.

He sat back in his cushioned chair, looking at me with frank eagerness.

"Okay," I repeated, searching back to how I should begin. "It's the earliest memory I have. I was three years old. . . ."

CHAPTER THREE
My First Dying

I *wanna cry. Can't. Can't make any sounds. Why is -- ?*

At three years old I didn't know there was a world out there. My world consisted of my mother's smooth round face, swirling brown hair, and distinctly robust voice; and my father's sad blue eyes, his darkly tanned features, so quiet-spoken; and my baby sister's unblinking brown eyes, crying with great wails or smiling with angelic bliss; and the blistered wrinkled faces of my grandfather and grandmother – my grandfather especially because he handed me chocolate kisses and his pressed lips made a soft buzzing sound as he watched me pop the chocolate into my mouth. Five others outside of me. At three years old I was content with that. That was my whole world.

Can't feel my arms or legs. I hear "Bigboy Bigboy Bigboy Bigboy." That me? No! Him Him Him – Let go! Mama! Bigboy won't let go –

What did I know of others? At three years old they weren't real to me. In my small world, when my stomach throbbed with hunger,

I was fed. When my body reeked from within, I was washed and dried. When I toppled over a toy fire truck and screamed with frenzied distress, Mama soothed me with her touch and her hearty voice hummed.

Mama brought me there, a concrete wading pool in a park. Later I learned its name: Willets Park. I've been there often since that day. Baby Sis was home with Gramps and Granma. Dada was working. Mama watched me as I sat beside a water spout, delighting in filling a plastic pail with water and spilling it out again.

A big boy in swimming trunks, perhaps nine years old, with swelling round cheeks, a thatch of unkempt black hair, and small eyes wide apart, waddled over and began talking to me. "Small fry," he called me. He grew annoyed when I didn't look up or answer him back. What did I know at three?

What did I know of others who enjoyed watching someone in distress? Or enjoyed squashing the helpless underfoot? What did I know of those who purposely caused pain? I didn't know of such things at three. All I knew were Mama, Dada, Baby Sis, Gramps and Granma. They were mindful of me. They were all that mattered.

At three, I didn't know I should be afraid.

Trees and sky swirled and came together. Mist drizzled over them and they were gone. "Mama!" I wanted to scream but couldn't. My throat was stopped. Something deflated within my chest, something that pushed out my final air. I gave one great heave of arms and legs. Then I was nothing.

How long? How long could it have been? Probably not long at all. At least, looking back, I didn't think so. But for a time there was nothing – not even blackness. No vision. No smells. No sound.

"Boy! You okay? Boy!" I didn't recognize the speaker. He spoke hoarsely, as if straining to keep his voice low but wanting to jolt me awake.

I felt a rumbling deep in my chest. It rose until I started coughing. My throat had opened and tears streamed down my face. I was lying on my back on the grass beside the wading pool. I stared up into the small eyes of an unfamiliar man. His face was pear-shaped and he had long wet streams of black hair. Black hair covered his chest and shoulders as well. His eyes were so far apart I could see only one at a time above me as he moved his head.

"I wan' Mama!" I cried out – almost screaming it.

"Shh," the man said. "Right here."

Mama's pale round face came into view. Her eyes were dark-rimmed and her lips quivered. She tried to form words but seemed unable to speak.

"Alex?" she whispered finally. I wanted to tell her not to cry. I made a weak attempt to smile up at her.

"He's okay," said the man. "No water in his lungs. He's okay."

I wanted to tell Mama about Big Boy. About his grabbing me in a headlock – but what did I know about headlocks? Big Boy had lifted me up, his thick fatty arm wrapped around my neck. I couldn't breathe. I couldn't find the ground. He held me there in the crook of his arm until –

"Mama!" I cried in gladness and tears.

"You'd better go!" she said urgently. Not to me. To *him*. To the man standing above me.

The stranger with the soaked black hair came close to Mama. His face, one bead-like eye, melted into Mama's face. They . . . came together. Then rushed apart.

"Go!" Mama said to him, brushing her slender fingers across his bare shoulders.

The man looked around and called, "Jaime! Let's go. Now!"

I rolled onto my side and watched Big Boy run off with the man. I tried to sit up on the grass.

"Mama?"

"What, Alex?'

"Big Boy hold me. He hold my head up. My feet high over the ground."

"Alex?" she said and hesitated. She looked toward the trees as if she was trying to remember something. She looked down at me. "Alex, nothing happened today. You played in the water with your pail. You're fine. You didn't see any 'Big Boy.' Okay?"

I was confused. But Mama repeated it, so earnestly that it seemed maybe it was true. Nothing had happened. There was no Big Boy.

But I remembered.

CHAPTER FOUR
A Friend on the Case

After I finished, we stared at each other. I pushed my eyeglasses back up my sweaty nose and he gave a nervous cough. I knew what he wanted to say – it was virtually exploding from his lips. But he didn't voice it.

After taking a long breath, my friend murmured, "So it started that long ago? When you were three?"

"Yes," I answered. "I began feeling the emotions of other people. I could look at someone and the feelings came at me. Like waves of heat."

"Alex, the man with your mother was *him*. He's the guy. Mr. Quiver."

That had already occurred to me. But the timing was off. The stranger at the park .would be too old to have been the same man who intervened on my behalf days ago.

"I don't think so," I said. "But the older boy back then would be about the right age."

14

My friend gave a shout of exclamation. "Jaime!" he cried out. "The boy's name! You said that's what the man called him. Jaime. His son."

"Yes. I remembered that name. All these years."

"You really think you were dead? That this Jaime held you so long that he strangled you to death?"

"I'm sure of it."

I looked away then, scanning my friend's office. We were in the Upper East Side of New York City and my friend had done well for himself. He was now Lawrence Coates, Attorney-at-law. Hard to believe he had once been scrawny Larry Coates with a silent 'e.' Hard to believe he was the twelve-year old I had met in Monticello when my parents rented a small diner there one special summer. It was Larry who first introduced me to Edgar Rice Burroughs and started me on the path to becoming a writer of science fiction.

"I can find him for you," Larry said, showing big white teeth in a smile that resembled the goofy grin he often had when I knew him long ago. "Your mother could tell us --"

"My mom's dead. She died in a car accident four years ago." I choked back anything further.

"Oh. Sorry." He picked up the handwritten note I had given him. "Maybe this guy's fingerprints are in the system. I'll try to --"

"I hoped you would, Larry. If he was careless enough. Let me know if you find anything."

"And what are you going to do? Don't do anything dangerous, Alex. I have people who can do the leg work. Follow people, ask questions, check backgrounds, the leg work. You know."

"Sure. That's what I expected you'd handle, Larry. I'm no hero."

I stood and we shook hands. He gazed down at his desk and I saw what he was thinking. He pulled out a large trade paperback from a desk drawer.

"One little favor, Alex." He gave me a lopsided grin. "Would you autograph this novel for me?"

"Which one is it?" I looked at the cover. "Oh. Evolved Parameters. My latest. Hope you've been enjoying it."

"Very much. I've been reading your stuff for a while now."

"That's always good to hear."

Larry handed me a pen and I found the title page. 'To Larry,' I wrote. 'Good friends are hard to come by. Let's make it easier from now on by staying in touch.' I signed it with elegant curves and swirls.

He read it silently, a broad smile on his face. "Thanks, Alex. I really appreciate this." He looked up and stared somberly at me. "It wouldn't make sense."

"What's that?" I asked.

"This guy . . . if it is that boy grown up . . . why would he leave a note and say he's watching you? After all these years, what could he possibly want?'

"I don't know, Larry."

As I reached the street, I felt a chill. I was scared out of my mind.

I saw 'Jaime' for only a brief moment when I was three. The stranger who helped me the other day didn't have to be the same person, either. It could have been some twisted fan. It could have been somebody else entirely. Anybody. Anybody at all.

CHAPTER FIVE
Incomplete People

These people around me. The outer surface is all they see. Outer clothes. Footwear. Body movement. Faces. They're so narrow in their perception of others. They know so little. They're so incomplete.

Usually I have to be familiar with people before I can read their hopes and desires. But this was an especially prescient day for me. Sharing the knowledge of my ability with my friend Larry Coates opened up my perception. Like anyone who wakes up to a bright sunny day feeling strong and healthy, my enhanced senses were remarkably acute.

I saw the truth in others as I walked down Lexington from Larry's office on East 67th Street before the evening rush. People. With so much hidden. But not from me.

I saw a middle-aged woman walking toward me in high-heels and short dress. She was thinking of an older man, her boss, and he was humping her on the couch in his office suite. Another person stepped into my line of sight, a man of about thirty, who saw himself stabbing a young woman – his wife? – to death.

Oh, not to worry. What I see in most people's minds aren't details of a real past history – that usually wouldn't be on their minds. No, frequently I receive images of their fantasies, their intentions. I see what people imagine, what they wish they could do. Most people daydream: they make love to or kill someone they obsess over. It's human nature.

To me, those people on the street seemed like lesser beings. Small, unrealized people that moved about in their own little worlds, oblivious to those who brush a sleeve or a leg against them. As I walked the crowded Manhattan Streets, I saw a compulsive liar walk by a child molester, a shoplifter pitch briefly against a corrupt business executive. I saw what they truly were beneath discreet lips, beneath noncommittal smiles, beneath bland faces. Inferior, ignorant beings.

Open wide for me.

I hadn't located anything like Mr. Quiver's intentions in the crowds that were around me. Probably because he wasn't following me. At least not then. He knew where I lived. Anyway, how would I distinguish his mind from the crowd? He knew I could read his mind. Knowing that meant he had a small measure of control. He showed me he could go blank when he rescued me from those two teenagers. He could also signal his presence by sending out his memory of me as a boy. Yes, he could do that. Knowledge is power.

Besides, *he* might not be out to get me. In the note, he wrote: "I don't intend hurting you. But I will be around to help again when you need it." There. You see. He was my fucking guardian angel. Okay, maybe he *was* that nine-year old Jaime who strangled me to death when I was a child. I was a boy of three back then and, last week, I saw the stranger only momentarily and under extreme duress. It's likely I didn't remember either one clearly. And even if he was the same person, what does he want?

I took a breath and gave a brief laugh. I'd been regarding all these incomplete people walking down Lex, living in their own small worlds – and here I was doing the same exact thing. Time to pretend I was one of them.

Subway station ahead. Walk down the stairs. Stand on the station platform. Look down tunnel. Roar and screech of a train coming in. Step into the packed car. Hold onto hanging handle. Smell the greasy coats and body odor of people brushing against you. Eyes looking upward, staring at nothing.

Standing in the subway car, I became one of them. Safe inside my own small world. Never mind that I saw into theirs as well. Made me a *complete* incomplete person, I suppose.

What should I think about?

Larry. Lawrence S. Coates, Attorney At Law. He was listed on the Web. Here in New York City. Coincidence? Probably. So I called. Spoke to the guy. Yes, he had lived in Monticello, New York as a boy. Who did I say I was? Yes, he remembered me. So I made the appointment. It was him, sure enough.

Monticello, about sixteen summers ago:

Larry was a boy about my age – I was twelve – he had a blonde crew-cut. I found him to be annoying from the start.

"My name's Larry Coates," said the kid with the crewcut. "That's Coates with an "e" in it but the "e" is silent."

Who cares? I thought.

19

"I've got some neat things in my basement," he went on eagerly. "I live right next door over there. I've got some old stuff that belonged to my father. He's dead now but he always told me I could have them. Real old books. Want to see?"

"What kind of books?" I asked. I'd been reading books on my own since I was little. I liked Hemingway's Nick Adams stories and I *really* liked Catcher in the Rye. My favorite books were ones that told of realistic people in real situations. *When I get older, I could be Holden Caulfield*! "How old are they?"

"Real old. Like a hundred years old. Wanna see?"

Dad had said that certain old things, like books and paintings, were priceless. I asked him, 'Does that mean they're not worth anything?' Dad had laughed and said, 'No. Just the opposite. They're worth so much that the owner wouldn't want to part with them. They're a treasure to the right person.'

Stacks of bent and warped hard covers were in piles in the Coates' basement -- pages torn or blotted with water stains, books with covers and bindings gone. Priceless all right – priceless, valueless, worthless junk.

I held up one remnant and looked at the boy, disappointed. "Is this it?"

He looked around the dimly lit basement. "Nooo . . . I was reading some books in the back, on that shelf."

He led me to a worn shelf and I picked up half a dozen ancient hard covers and looked at the titles. I recognized some, like Wuthering Heights and A Tale of Two Cities. I turned to the page with the publishing dates -- Mom told me about publishing dates and what that meant in the books she brought home from the library -- and saw that these had been reprinted numerous times.

And then there was one . . .

"Is this . . ?" I found myself breathless with excitement. "Is this like from the movies? Does this book come from those Tarzan movies?"

Larry laughed. "No, 'course not. The books came first. Long time ago."

I looked at the publishing date. "Copyright Edgar Rice Burroughs, Inc., 1924. This is in pretty good shape. Are any pages missing?"

"No. I don't think so."

"<u>Tarzan and the Ant Men</u>. That wasn't made into a movie, was it?"

"Nope."

I opened the book to a random page and read:

> Tarzan grappled them with his fingers, tearing the riders from their mounts. One rider, leaping straight for him, struck his legs and sides.
>
> Again and again the needlelike points of their rapiers pierced the ape-man's hide until he was red with his own blood.

(Note: For those of you concerned about copyright infringement, this is the proper attribution for this novel – Burroughs, Edgar Rice, <u>Tarzan and the Ant Men,</u> New York: Grosset & Dunlap, 1924, pp. 125-126.)

"Who is this guy?" I asked. "Edgar Rice Burroughs?"

"Some writer from the Midwest. He died a long time ago. My father told me that this Burroughs never even traveled to Africa. He made everything up. And not only that! Burroughs wrote a whole other series of novels called the Barsoom series."

"Barzoom?" I imagined some otherworldly sorcerer. "Who's Barzoom?"

"Barsoom! With an 's.' It's not a who! It's Mars. The planet Mars. That's what the Martians called their planet."

Angrily, I held the flat of the book close to Larry's face. "How could this guy know anything about Martians and what they called their planet?"

He laughed, feeling superior. "He didn't. Burroughs made it all up. Made it up out of his own head."

I was shocked. For the first time it occurred to me that a writer could make up whole civilizations through imagination alone.

"Mr. Brocton?"

Back in the subway car. The buffeting passage of the train and the crashing of metal on metal brought me back to reality. I turned to the man who spoke. He was a short man, bald, with a smear of a black mustache plastered to his upper lip. His eyes were dark brown, now wide with a look of awe. He was dressed in a worn gray suit, his dull blue tie hanging askew from his neck.

"You are Alex Brocton," he said. "The sci fi writer?"

"Yes?"

"I recognized you from the book jacket of your latest novel. I'm in the middle of it. Can't put it down."

I sensed his enthusiasm. His mind, however, was projecting a tall, attractive, red-haired woman who stroked his bald head. She didn't come from my novel. His wife? A secret girlfriend? I couldn't tell.

"You're reading <u>Evolved Parameters</u>?" I asked.

"That's the one," he answered. "Too bad I don't have it with me. I'd ask for your autograph. It's the best book I've read in a long time. Where do you get your ideas?"

"Schenectady. That's just a joke. A fellow writer is famous for saying that." I saw that this little guy was expecting a better response. "Much of it comes from my own experience. Just a bit twisted and turned around."

I shuddered without reason when the little man touched my coat sleeve.

"Do you always write from your own experience?" he asked. "Those adventures in the novel are so outrageous. Even when they seem realistic. Know what I mean?"

I wasn't sure I did. In his mind, he was in bed with a voluptuous blonde. Again, not connected with anything in <u>Evolved Parameters</u>. It made me somewhat unsettled that this man could talk about one thing but think something completely different at the same time.

"Do you mean," I began, my mind hunting up creative juices. "that Daya's conflict with the blue goddess didn't seem real to you?"

"Hmm. I don't know. When did he find the blue goddess?"

"Early on. Right after Maeorin confronted Daya about his purpose for traveling in the Nebulan Lifestream. That was in Chapter Two."

"Oh, sure. Well that propels the story, doesn't it? Something had to happen." The train came to a stop. "Well, this is my station. Good talking to you, Mr. Brocton."

The little man shoved his way past the other passengers. He cleared the doors and they closed. He was gone. I stood there, gripping the post tightly, ready to scream.

I knew he hadn't read my book. There were no blue goddess, no Nebulan Lifestream, no Maeorin, and no Daya. I made all of it up. But that wasn't what left me in shock. It was what he was thinking when he looked back at me just before pushing through the opened doors. It was the clear image of another woman clad in a green bathing suit, her black hair dripping and hanging wildly.

The young woman was someone he knew. My mother.

CHAPTER SIX
The One Who Should Know

Mom in a green bathing suit. Dripping wet. Smiling.

I don't think I ever saw her in a bathing suit. Not like that. She looked so young. So . . . It had to be before I was born.

Damn disturbing.

How could that mustached pipsqueak have that image in his head? How did he know her? Who was he?

I sat on the bus heading down Jewel Avenue toward my apartment, chewing on my lip in worry the whole way. So many damn questions.

The sun was low in the horizon when I reached my second-floor garden apartment. I pulled out my cell phone, and dropped heavily onto the couch, worn through with fatigue and despair.

I couldn't stop thinking about that little mustached man and his fake replies about my book.

Someone must've put him up to it, coming to me like that. Mr. Quiver? Maybe it's more than one person. Right. A conspiracy. Do I sound paranoid, or what? But why signal me that they're watching? And why are THEY doing this? Who are THEY?

I punched in my favorites on my cell and stared at the name and phone number for a long time.

Should I call? How could I put it to him? Would he even know? But he's the only one who could possibly know!

Without having any idea what I would say, I pressed the tab and heard the phone ringing. He picked up the phone at his end after two rings.

"Hello?" It was his usual soft, querying voice.

"Dad? Hi. It's me. Alex."

"Alex? Everything all right?"

"Yeah. Everything's okay." I waited for Dad to say something. Then, I put in, "It's getting cold outside, though. We might get an early snow."

"I wish you'd come down to North Miami for a visit. It's seventy-five degrees and sunny today."

"Maybe I will. I've got that big convention in Philly this coming weekend. I've been pretty busy. But maybe this winter." Silence on the other end. I thought I could feel Dad's disappointment but, of course, it wasn't possible for me to sense feelings over the phone. "Dad? I've got to ask you something."

He took so long to say anything that I almost called out "Dad?" but then he said in his quiet manner, "Go ahead. Ask."

"It's about Mom." Still nothing coming from the other end. *Did he know something was up?* "Do you know if Mom was seeing someone before you got married?"

"Your mother was an attractive girl. She was going out with lots of boys in college. Even when we started dating. Why are you asking?"

"Well, do you . . . do you know if she kept in touch with any of them?"

"Alex, what are you getting at? What's going on?"

What should I tell him? How far can I go? This was for real, now. "Well . . . you see . . ." *That's right. Drag it out so it becomes impossible to –* "I'm being followed. By two different people it seems. They accosted me –"

"Are you hurt, Alex? Did they hurt you?"

"No, no. By 'accosted' I mean they came up to me, talked. I got a note saying they wanted to help me. That they'd be watching. The note was signed 'Mr. Quiver.' Ever hear that name before?"

Again, the long silence. Then, "Mr. Quiver? You saw that written down?"

"Yeah, Dad. I have the note." I saw no reason to explain that I turned the note over to Larry Coates. The air was tense enough as it was.

"It said 'Mr. Quiver?'" Dad's voice came in staccato breaths. "You're sure?"

"Yeah, Dad. Of course. Does that mean something to you?" A very long silence. "Dad! You still there?"

"I'm here. Look, it's surprising to me that anyone would know about it. You haven't heard that name before, have you? Your mother hadn't told you the story, had she?"

"No," I answered, a bit shocked by this turn around. "What story?"

"Your mother told me about Mr. Quiver so many years ago, I hadn't thought about it until you said it."

Then, he stopped. Silence once more. I was getting impatient. Why did it bother him so much?

Finally, "Ruthie was a little girl. Her mother, Josephine, came into her room one night and found Ruthie on her bed, crying. Her mother asked her about it. Ruthie told her that Uncle George had been scaring her. George was Josephine's brother; your mother's uncle. Let me see . . . your mother would've been only eight or, maybe, nine years old. George was much younger than Ruthie's mother. He'd be around seventeen at the time."

Yes! I remembered! I knew Uncle George when I was a child. Lost touch long ago and hadn't thought of him since.

"So what did George do?"

"He was remarkably good at hand shadows."

"What?"

"Hand shadows. You know. Using his hands to form shadows on the wall. Whenever he visited his sister, he would entertain by casting shadows on the wall. The thing is, when he sat alone with Ruthie, he would change the shadows. He liked to scare Ruthie."

"What do you mean? How'd he change them?"

"Well, this is how Ruthie explained it. In front of her mother and others, George would cast the shadow of a rabbit or a boy's face. With Ruthie alone, that same rabbit would turn into a goat with a beard and horns, its mouth animated to bite. The shadow of the boy's face would become an old man gnashing his teeth. George had a way of making these shadows hideous. It was a part of Uncle George that Ruthie described as 'malicious.'"

"So, where does Mr. Quiver come in?"

"From Ruthie's mother. Your mother said that Josephine made up that name and suggested it to George. Josephine was incensed that her baby brother could do this to her child. She left Ruthie's room for several minutes and returned, dragging George by the arms. Josephine made George apologize. But even more, she made him tell Ruthie something she never forgot."

Listening to Dad on my cell, the hairs on my arms stood up.

"Uncle George said – and this is as close as I can remember Ruthie's story – 'You don't have to be afraid of shadows. I'm leaving a special shadow with you, Ruthie, one that will protect you from any of the other shadows. It's called 'Mr. Quiver.' I'm giving Mr. Quiver to you and though you can't see him, he'll always watch over you.'

"Ruthie recalled staring wide-eyed at Uncle George and her mother and feeling her fears lift and float away. That's exactly how she described it. And she smiled, the same smile she gave me when she finished telling me the story. I'd always believed it was something she never told anyone else. So, that's where Mr. Quiver came from."

Dad left me grasping for meaning while he was silent again. I hadn't heard so many words from him in years, and his still voice now left me tingling.

"So Uncle George was Mr. Quiver," I muttered. "He could be behind this. Watching out for me. How old would he be now?" Nothing from the other end of the line. "Dad?"

"It isn't George."

"Why not?"

"George died in a plane crash about two years ago. At least, that's when I received notice about it from a lawyer. Uncle George and his wife, Florence, were killed when his chartered jet crashed in the mountains in New Mexico. There were no survivors. But . . ."

He left me hanging again. "But what, Dad?"

"He had a son. Howard."

"I remember Howard."

"Oh?"

"He punched me in the face when I was a boy."

"He did? Where was I?"

"I don't remember, Dad. Maybe you were working."

"Why did he punch you?"

"It was over a quarter. I dropped it on the sidewalk in front of our home and Howard picked it up. He was a lot older than me. At least ten years older, I think. He picked it up and put it in his pocket. I asked for it back and he refused. I tried to reach into his pocket and he punched me. I got a bloody nose out of it. Never did get my quarter. As far as I know, that was the last time I saw him. That's when they moved away."

Dad was silent for several beats. Then, "I didn't know that happened, Alex. I wonder if your mother knew, if she saw it. When George and Florence moved to Florida, we didn't see much of them at all. Only, Ruthie spoke to them on the phone from time to time."

"So, Dad, you're saying George and his wife died two years ago?"

"Yes. That's when their lawyer called me. Terrible thing."

"How old would that make Cousin Howard?"

"He would be in his thirties. Maybe close to forty by now. When his parents died, he was living in New Jersey. I talked to him on the phone when I found out about his parents." In the long pause, I imagined Dad reflecting on Mom and those lost relatives. Dad continued, "I hadn't seen Howard in such a long time. I don't have any idea what he looks like now."

There! There it was. The connection.

"Dad," I said, excitement rising in me. "The little man with the mustache in the subway car. That was Howard!"

"If it is," Dad said, his voice deliberate, "then you have to wonder why he's contacting you this way. Why is he playing this game of 'Mr. Quiver?'"

Dad was echoing my thoughts. I shared my own: "And what is he really after?"

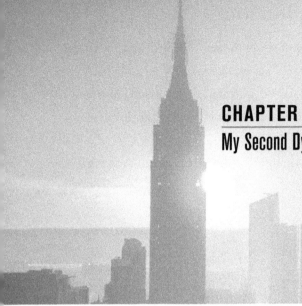

CHAPTER SEVEN
My Second Dying

Tingling touched my eyes, white-hot and coal black. It became flame, it became scalding, it became a searing agony and I opened my mouth to scream . . .

I woke up with a start, my face soaked with sweat. I breathed rapidly, searching in the dark. Middle of the night. I caught glimpses of light from the street coming through my window. I could see, I could see.

Ever have a nightmare so real that you saw every detail, heard every sound, even wished for it to end but it didn't? Well, I did that night after speaking to Dad about cousin Howard. I dreamt something that was so real . . .

. . . I opened my mouth to scream and it was worse, the scorching pain became unbearable, and I tried to scream but nothing rose from my lips and I cried and my tears were hot flares pressed against my open unseeing eyes . . .

Sitting up in my bed, breathing heavily, taking in the bits of light in the night, I realized it was only a dream. But it wasn't only a dream. It really happened. It was the second time I was almost killed. Except I hadn't died. But living through it was worse.

It happened years ago when I was a teenager. Mom and Dad rented a small diner in Monticello for the summer. I was helping out, busing tables, helping with the dishes:

"Why de' hell don'cha?" asked the man staring across the counter at Dad.

I saw the guy as I came out of the kitchen carrying a rubber tub to gather dishes. I'd never seen him before. He was taller than Dad, younger, with a couple of days' growth of whiskers on his face. His brown hair was messy and hanging over his forehead. He wore a dirty tee shirt and old black jeans that was torn in places. The man made me feel a growing dread.

"C'mon, mister," the stranger growled. "I gotta take a pee. Where the hell do *you* go to pee, huh?"

Dad stood behind the counter trying to act calm. He wasn't – not inside. I felt Dad's nervousness flaring hotly.

Mom was taking orders and I was rushing between clearing tables and the kitchen. Turning to look back, I saw Frank Shaye, our friend and Dad's partner, through the swinging doors. Frank's being there comforted me. He stood on a platform, a semi-circular counter around him, preparing food in steaming containers. Frank had been driving up to help every morning for more than a week, leaving again right after cleaning up. We needed him and he knew it. Business was good.

"I'm very sorry," Dad said to the man at the counter, "but this place doesn't have plumbing facilities for the shop."

"Tha's crazy! Hey, man, I gotta go. I'll do it right here if I gotta."

By this point everyone was watching the stranger and I felt their fear. Dad had to do something. Quickly.

"Look," Dad came around the counter to talk quietly. "Let me check with my wife over there. If it's okay with her, you can use our private bathroom in the back."

"Yeah. Do that!" said the man, grinning with yellowed teeth.

"Just give me a minute."

Dad spoke to Mom in whispers.

As I cleaned a table, I glanced at the man. He was giving off contradictory feelings. It jarred me. *All wrong,* I thought. *People who have to pee show it. This guy's relaxed. He doesn't have to go. He's getting ready for something.*

The man stood looking at the customers, giving them a reassuring smile. *An empty smile,* I sensed. *A dead smile.*

Something was very wrong.

I edged my way toward Mom and Dad standing between tables in the crowded shop. "Dad?" I said.

"Not now, Alex."

The stranger leaned against the counter. He fixed his eyes on me, stopped smiling, and pressed his lips together.

"I suppose . . ." Mom was saying.

"Don't, Mom," I said sharply. People at the near tables looked up at me. "At least get Frank out here," I tried to whisper. "Something's wrong."

Dad intervened. "Alex, it's okay. I'll take him. He'll be out of here in a minute."

Dad didn't know what I was sensing and I didn't know how to explain it to him. He went to the guy, smiled, and led the way to our bedrooms in the back.

"Alex," Mom said, "get those tables cleared. We've got customers waiting."

I went quickly, clashing dishes together as I dropped them into the tub. I ran into the kitchen, dropped the tub by the dishwasher, and hurried to the back rooms.

The stranger was in our bathroom while Dad stood further behind talking to Aly at the open back door.

I stayed by the bathroom door. I couldn't sense anything. After a moment, I heard the toilet flush. I could hear running water in the sink. A few seconds later, the door creaked as it slowly opened.

The stranger was looking upward and didn't see me. What I felt coming from him was a swirling tornado. Dry rather than wet. Brittle rather than flowing. I hadn't felt such a thing before. Years later I knew: It was calculated brutal indifference.

He stepped forward, pivoting to turn toward Dad. He moved the door closed and I saw the gun in his hand. It was small and flat, easily hidden. It almost looked like a toy. The man lifted it and pointed at Dad.

He wants to kill everybody! I realized. *Dad, Mom, Alyson, anyone in sight.*

I stood there, shaking with sudden hot terror.

I leapt and clamped down on his arm, all teeth and nails, animal-like. The stranger screamed.

I was swept dizzily by the guy's powerful arm but I held on firmly. People running toward me, the sound of cries and yells, drifted around me in a haze. I kept my eyes on one thing – that small flat gun.

With his other hand, he punched me twice in the side of my face. I felt numb but stayed focused. I fought to get my fingers on the gun. I dug my nails into the hand holding the trigger. He shoved me hard against a wall as he fell against it. I felt people grabbing for me as they grappled with the man. He was so strong they couldn't drag him away from me.

Pressed against the wall by the guy's arm, I was pinned at my upper chest. I was losing my breath as my grip on his arm – both teeth and hands – slipped. I couldn't hold on much longer.

Several people had the man tightly in their grasp but he was all will, all force. I saw the gun tilt toward me – it was the only thing he could move. I no longer had any breath and my eyes blurred with tears.

I lost my grip. My hand on the gun slid away. I saw the barrel of the gun twisting to face me. Suddenly, I was somewhere else, watching this happen to another young boy, not to me. But then I was back. Right there. I saw the man's finger squeeze the trigger.

My face was ablaze and I gave a silent scream as the fire ripped into my eyes and nose and mouth. The smell of firecrackers and a single brilliant flash overwhelmed me. I was shattered with the pain.

The only thing left to me was an expanding whiteness that didn't end.

When I awoke in the hospital, I couldn't see a thing.

CHAPTER EIGHT
A Wish for Sight

I had a fitful night's sleep, images of that crazed man and my struggling with him over the gun still in my thoughts. I must've dozed sometime in the early morning hours and I finally awoke around nine-thirty. No need to rush to some office for work. The advantage of being a well-paid independent author.

I took off my glasses and stared at my face in the bathroom mirror as I threw warm water on it. A young face. A twenty-eight year old face. Two-days growth of whiskers on it. I lathered shaving cream over the whiskers and put razor to face.

My mother's eyes gazed back at me, large and brown, full head of brown hair. My father's strong jaw with a deep cleft in the chin. The shape of my head leaner and more narrow than either of my parents. A crease on each side of my angular cheeks showing as I stretched my lips. Entirely my own. A young face. My face.

Eyes curious. Eyes that held a look of false innocence. They had seen things that most people don't get to see. Things not pleasant, not innocent, things that were not talked about but instead kept hidden in one's darkest thoughts. When had that started? After I came out of my blindness. After I fought that maniac with the gun. After he fired it into the air next to my face. After the burning. I was a thirteen year old when that happened. A scared young boy with my eyes bandaged, not knowing if I would ever see again. I was in the hospital. . . .

The world was closing in on me. I was being squeezed, unable to take a full breath. I felt perspiration slide down my back, wondering if I would ever see anything outside of this blackness surrounding me.

Where's Dr. Ackerman? I wondered.

"Frank said we made out a little ahead from where we started," Dad said.

He had been wheeled into my room and had been talking with Mom about the snack shop. Dad had suffered a minor heart attack during the incident that put me in the hospital. Mention of Frank Shaye was meant to include me in the conversation. Frank, who had rescued me six years before when I became hopelessly lost, had to go back to the city. However, he had asked Dad to call him as soon as the bandages came off. My sister Alyson was with us and I heard her sniffling every so often.

Where are you, Doctor --?

"That's true, Alex," Mom said, and patted my arm. "We didn't do as well as we would have if we finished the summer, but we're pleased with what we earned." I could sense that she was putting on a false cheerfulness for my sake.

Why is Dr. Ackerman taking so long? She said she was removing the bandages this morning. Why isn't she here?

"What are we going to do?" I asked. I wanted to add '*if I'm blind?*'

Dad said, "We'll take you home, of course."

"I'm not going back to the snack shop."

"No, you're not. We've closed it up and cancelled our lease. When you're released from the hospital, we're going back home. We'll finish the summer there."

But what if I can't see? What do I do when school starts again? How do I go to classes? How do I read books? How do I play my video games? What about my friends? Mom? Dad? What am I supposed to do?

"In another week," Dad said, "I'll be able to drive a cab again. I called Lou and he says my job is waiting for me."

"Oh, Alex, Alex!" Aly called out. I heard her stomp up to my bed. "Dad's getting his job back delivering for Stafford's Bakery. Tell Alex, Daddy."

Dad laughed and it felt good to hear him.

"Seems to me you just did, Baby. But Alyson's right. I got a letter in the mail from the new owners. I'm to report back to Stafford's on the first of October. And I'll be getting a higher salary."

Mom said, "Until then, we'll have to make ends meet. I'm thinking of working part time at Jaffre's Diner. Now that I have some experience."

If – I considered – *If you don't have to stay home with a blind kid!*

"But, Mom," I started, hearing the whine in my own voice and wishing I didn't have to say it. "What happens if --"

"Hello," interrupted a hard female voice. It was Dr. Ackerman. "Sorry to have taken so long."

I sat up. "How could you do that? Don't you know how hard it is to sit here waiting to get these bandages off? Don't you know how scared I've been?"

Silence for a long moment.

I suddenly realized that, of course, it wasn't my place to yell at a doctor. I was a kid, after all.

"Alex," Dr. Ackerman said, "I was with another patient. Sorry if it inconvenienced you." Annoyed, I wanted to answer her when she continued, "I was with a twelve-year old girl named Lizzie. She needed me to be with her."

I felt the shame wash over me. How could I have been so unkind? So insensitive? I should have been able to read the doctor's feelings – I might've if I had taken a second -- but how could I possibly have known?

"Are you able to help her?" I asked.

"She passed away a few minutes ago."

I tried to say something, more than once, but I choked each time.

Dr. Ackerman moved to the side of my bed. I tried to read her feelings but my way was blocked by a solid wall. She wasn't letting anything in. Something metallic clanged on the small table next to me.

"Okay, Alex, sit back, now." She pressed my shoulder and eased me back. "Mrs. Brocton," – her voice projected away from me -- "would you shut the light, please?" I heard Mom's footsteps and the soft click of the light switch. "Stay perfectly still, Alex. I'm cutting the bandages just behind your left ear." She went to work.

The light came through as the first layer dropped off. I took a deep breath in relief. Then the doctor removed the second layer. I saw the window and part of a wall and the vague movement of people in the room. It was as if I were looking through a sheet of cracked ice.

My chest felt leaden and I was sickened with fear. "Why can't I see?"

"It's okay," Mom said. "You've got some thick ointment covering your eyes."

Dr. Ackerman said, "That's right. I'll wipe it off in a bit. I want you to take a minute, Alex. Keep your eyes open. Take in the light around you."

My heart lifted as I took another careful look around. "I can make out the window. I see the sunlight through the Venetian blinds. I can see the bed and the chairs. I see Aly and you, Mom, and Dad. I see you, Doctor. You're all just outlines, kind of fuzzy, but I can see you. Can't you get this gook off me now?"

"Yes, Alex. Lie still."

She gently rubbed my eyes with a thin soft cloth. I could feel flecks of dried cream come off. And then . . .

Daylight. Morning. Lifelight. THE WORLD!

Dr. Ackerman came in front of me, obscuring everything else. "Alex, I want you to focus on my finger. Follow it with your eyes. Don't move your head."

Her finger was almost edgeless, seeming to have several different thicknesses at the same time. Still, I had no trouble keeping my eyes on it as it moved left and right.

"That's good. Very good."

She stepped back and I had my first full look at Dr. Ackerman. Her features were indistinct but I made out her brushed-back short hair, large dark eyes beneath sharply-drawn eyebrows, wide dimpled cheeks, and the folds of a double chin.

Dr. Ackerman was a middle-aged lady who bulged out of her medical smock.

And hers was the most beautiful face I ever saw.

41

CHAPTER NINE
Strange Talent

"**A**bout this Mr. Quiver," Larry was saying over the phone, "I'm not sure what we can do about him once we find him. I mean, he hasn't broken any laws. We've got nothing to arrest him for. He hasn't done anything to you."

"Yes, I realize that." I grimaced at my cell phone. At that particular moment, I wanted to strangle Larry Coates. I suddenly remembered that he had a talent for stating the obvious. Still, I had to acknowledge that I probably needed to hear the thought spoken aloud. Yes, I needed to hear it. And yet it was totally annoying to hear him say it. Into the phone, I said evenly, "I simply want to find him and ask why he's watching me. I need to know what his intentions are."

"Okay, Alex. But you got me confused here. Do you think this cousin of yours, Howard, is Mr. Quiver? Or is he the stranger who helped you when those two teenagers tried to mug you? Who's in charge of this thing?"

"I don't know."

"Okay. Not much help, but okay. What's your cousin's last name?"

"Schuyler. That's my mother's maiden name. I assume that's his also. Howard Schuyler."

"And he's somewhere in New Jersey?"

"That's what my dad thinks. At least that's where he was living when Uncle George, his father, died two years ago."

"Okay. If he's still living in New Jersey, I'll find him. How old would you say he is?"

"Just by looks? I'd say he's in his thirties. Maybe close to forty."

"Okay. I'll call you when I got something definite. Get back to me if you run into either of those guys."

"Of course. Thanks, Larry."

"There's something else."

"What?"

"You know stuff. Stuff that people are thinking. More than just seeing things in people's faces. When you were in my office, you saw something in my mind, right? You knew I wanted you to autograph my book even before I took it out. Didn't you?"

God, he was annoying. "You might say that."

"I am saying that. Something happened to you the summer we spent together in Monticello. When you were nearly shot. It changed you."

"Being almost shot would change anybody."

"You know what I mean. You see things in people. You got a strange talent because your eyes were damaged. Maybe it was trauma, too. When I visited you in the hospital afterward, you looked like you knew things – even when your eyes were bandaged.

And I think those glasses you wear help you in some way, too. Don't they?"

I sighed. "What do you want to know?"

"Everything. What is it you do? I mean, what's the extent of it? How did you find out you can see what's in people's minds? Can you see into my mind right now?"

"No, I can't. I have to be near you. Proximity matters. Besides, I don't see anything though the phone. It's a mechanical device."

"What did you do? I mean, how did you first discover you had this talent?"

So I told him. Not everything. I decided from the start that some things were none of Larry's business. So I began . . .

"I didn't want to wear glasses. Mom and the eye doctor picked them. Big round black frames. Impossible to miss. Especially by the other kids in school.

"'You need that wide a frame,' Dr. Boylan said, 'for peripheral vision.'

"*I need that wide a frame,* I thought, *so that every girl in my class will have a good laugh when they see me.*

"When the optician fitted me for them, Mom stood behind me, guarding me so I couldn't bolt out of my seat. The whole idea of wearing glasses sickened me.

"'Take a look, Alex,' Dr. Boylan said. 'You'll be surprised.'

"I took a look. I wasn't surprised. I stared back at giant insect eyes.

"'These things make my eyes look huge – I look like a squirrel. A rabid squirrel.'

"Mom leaned down and turned my chair to gaze at me. She assessed me like a talent scout studying an actor. 'Intelligent-looking. Studious.'

"'No, Mom. Fish-eyed. Dopey.'

"'Alex, you're just making a joke of it. You look handsome.'

"'It makes me look like a fool, Mom. Do I have to wear them?'

"'Only if you want to see,' said Dr. Boylan.

"I glared at the doctor and then turned pleadingly to Mom.

"Something changed in Mom's face. She suddenly seemed younger. Hair neatly brushed, cheeks smoothed with cream, a hint of bluish eye shadow. Just as suddenly, the shoulders and back of a man's head shot into view in front of her."

In present time, Larry intervened: "Was that your father? When he was younger, too? I bet your mom was daydreaming. And you caught them in the act by peeping into her thoughts, right?"

"Not exactly. Let me go on, will you?"

I didn't fill Larry in on the following: I couldn't see the man's face but he wasn't shaped anything like Dad. He was heavier and rounder than Dad. The man wasn't wearing a shirt and what I saw of Mom's shoulders was bare, too. She moved and there was a bit of breast and naked thigh . . .

"I saw that she wasn't fully dressed," I said into the phone. "She was trying on some new clothes she was buying."

Larry drew in a breath at the other end of the phone. "So you saw her naked trying on a dress? That's what she was thinking?"

"Yeah. But I didn't see much. Can I go on?"

"Do you think women do a lot of daydreaming about trying on dresses?"

"Larry!"

"Okay, Alex. Go on. I'm all ears."

"Then she was Mom again, looking worriedly back at me. Her face pale, lips severe, wisps of hair hanging over her forehead. 'Are you all right?' she asked.

"I was silent for a few seconds, trying to figure out what I had seen."

What I didn't say into the phone to Larry: *Was that really Mom NAKED? Where in my sick crazy mind did I come up with that? THAT WASN'T MOM! Not in a million years! Couldn't be. Had to be something I saw on TV. An actress that looked like Mom. Why would it even be in my head NOW?*

Back to the story I was telling Larry: "I looked at my mom and said, 'No, I'm not all right. I've got a headache from these *damn eyeglasses.*'

"Dr. Boylan took my glasses away, examined them under some kind of scope, and returned with them. 'They shouldn't cause headaches. They're adjusted perfectly to your eyes. Nothing wrong with the lenses that I can see. Try them again.'

"I put them on and leaned forward to see myself in the mirror. My immense eyes frowned back at me. Rabid squirrel eyes.

"'Let's see,' said Mom.

"I looked up at her, fearful that I would see her undressing to try on something else. Mom surveyed my face.

"I avoided focusing on her, gazing instead at the light fixture above. *Not curious. Don't want to know.*

"'Nice glasses,' Mom said. 'Very fashionable – and you look good in them.'

"'Okay, Mom. You win.' I gave her a faint smile.

"We left the place and went to our car. While Mom drove, I peered at her. I *was* curious. I *did* want to know – would I see Mom that way again? Was it my imagination? Where did I get such an idea?

"'You'll see,' she was saying. 'You'll get used to wearing them in no time.' She gave me a sideways glance. 'Alex? What is it?'

"I hesitated until the car veered off-lane. 'Mom, watch the road.'

"She recovered, eyes front. 'Why were you looking at me like that?'

"What could I tell her? How could I explain something that I didn't understand myself?"

"What was it, Alex?" Larry interrupted again. "What did you see that time?"

"Shut up a minute! I'm telling you what it was: Nothing happened when I looked at Dr. Boylan. But it just happened again, when I concentrated on Mom. I didn't know why.

"What I saw was – the face of a man who looked half-familiar – with his shirt off.'"

This time I told all to Larry. In Larry's office, I had already revealed my mom's infidelity. "He had a broad face, a dark jumble of hair, and small eyes very far apart. I knew I had seen him before, many years ago. He was standing, leaning into Mom, his arms around her naked back, kissing her long and hard."

"Mr. Quiver," Larry muttered on his end.

"I didn't know that name then. Besides, I told you, it's more likely that the man who helped me was his son."

"Yeah. I remember. So what did you say to your mother?"

"I told her: 'I'm just trying to concentrate on things, trying to get used to these eyeglasses.' The way she looked, I knew she wasn't satisfied with that. 'For a second there, I thought I saw a big spider climbing up your shoulder. That's all.'

"She gave a short laugh of relief. 'Well, I suppose that could happen,' she replied. 'Until you get used to looking through glasses, you might have a few problems seeing things clearly. Give it time.'

"'Yeah. Okay.' I answered.

"I sat back in the passenger seat and closed my eyes."

"That's it?" asked Larry. "End of conversation?"

"Yes. End of conversation. But I couldn't stop thinking about it. Actually, I didn't know what to think. Remember, it was all new to me back then. The most distressing thing about it was that I knew I *hadn't* imagined it. Not that second time in the car. And, another thing: it wasn't coming from *my* mind. I felt that real strong. I hadn't thought that image up. It had come from *outside* of me."

"So," Larry began, "you knew. You had seen it in her mind and you realized it. You've been able to do that ever since."

"Yes, I knew. That's when it started. And my glasses seem to help. I see people's thinking – some of it – with my glasses on. I need to be able to see clearly for me to visualize it."

I finished my call with Larry then.

Now Larry knew.

And I wasn't feeling particularly happy about it. Not at all.

CHAPTER TEN
My Writing Life

As a famous writer, I've led a highly glamorous life. Beautiful women have traipsed in and out of my apartment at all hours (I AM a bachelor besides being world-renowned); been feted with luxurious banquets by many influential giants of politics and industry; handed wagonloads of money for making appearances at bookstores and hotel grand ballrooms. I've lived a cushy life of grandeur, wealth, and indulgence.

Bullshit!

Like most mornings, this day I was sitting at the computer battling for words on a screen. It was as lonely a period of time as any author has ever described. But it was also the most absorbing, most imaginative, and most vitalizing time I could spend.

My protagonist WAS like me but he was also quite different. He faced situations that had certain similarities to what I have faced but, then again, they diverged drastically. My characters were real to me but they also grew out of my head with mythological spontaneity. I created whole worlds in an instant. I was, very simply, a world shaper.

My latest novel, still unfinished, was entitled <u>Symbiote Sight.</u> My main character, a twenty-something restaurant manager, discovered that he had an extraterrestrial entity living inside him. Uh oh! Hope I didn't just give too much away.

Typing on my keyboard, I lost myself in that made-up world, reworking the specific details in chapter two of my (brilliant!) tome. Okay, so many science fiction writers have told about aliens taking over humans – and I'm terrified that I'm rehashing old material – but I had a fresh insight and a theme never explored before (I hoped). So, there I was, absorbed in words on a computer screen, unaware subjectively of passing time, while, all the same, completely aware objectively, going through my paces:

Dull throbbing pain drew him into wakefulness. The ache increased and began pounding inside his head. He tried to will it away, but it persisted and grew.

"What are you trying to do to me?" he wanted to scream. But his lips trembled imperceptibly and no sound emerged. He tried again: "Go away. Let me sleep."

It squeezed inside his head

No, no good. Didn't sound right. Not "squeezed." Maybe . . .

It shuffled in his mind, scratching hard at something

What "something?" Too vague! Got to be more specific. What? WHAT??

. . . scratching hard at soft tissue deep
within. The pain was excruciating and he screamed
soundlessly again. He drew in short breaths. Air
passed into his lungs. Calm enveloped him as it
settled into quiet, wrapping itself

"It? Itself? Was that enough?" I mulled it over. Sitting back, my
mind raced over remembered images of other people's thoughts I
had previously caught. Wishes and hopes I had once picked out of
individuals' heads as they passed me on the streets of New York.
Knowing these weren't MY thoughts, I culled through them, seeking
just the right form I needed. Okay. Sure. I was fully capable of coming
up with ideas in my own experience. Naturally. But I also liked to
evaluate other perspectives outside of myself and use them in my
writing. An added resource, you know? That was fair, wasn't it? Or was
it cheating? Maybe. But maybe not. I still provided my own words.

. . . wrapping its wormy essence about his
brain. Air continued to encompass him as his
eyelids fluttered, bringing him back to this
world.
"Doctor Bryan. He's coming out of it." A
feminine voice, sharp and deep.

Shades of Dr. Ackerman who ministered over my twelve-year
old self when I was temporarily blinded. You see? I drew on my own
experience, too.

A long movement of white crossed his vision.
Warm fingers gently plied open one eye, then the
other. His head felt spongy, but when he opened

his eyes, they focused immediately on the two figures above him.

"Mr. Sarker," said the male figure in white.

He stared up into the doctor's face, noting deep lines, a drooping gray mustache, unkempt silver hair. His own cold lips trembled, wanting to question the doctor. So many questions. "Yes?" he said.

"Mr. Sarker. You've been in a coma. Do you remember what happened?"

He remembered. His body shook with the memory, remembering explosion after explosion close to his ear. He remembered the tightening pull of the rope around his wrists and ankles. He remembered the greasy turpentine smell of the cloth thrust into his mouth so that he could barely breathe. He remembered the coarse illiterate voices of the young men (there were three) hovering above him as he stared at the dirt-smudged linoleum floor. He remembered the hard metal barrel of the pistol pressed against the back of his head. . . .

He wanted to say it all. Tell this doctor everything he remembered. "Yes," he managed.

The nurse leaned forward, touching his hand with her carefully firm touch.

"Rest now. You'll have time to talk later."

He stared up into her cool

Her cool what? Eyes, of course. Blue? Too clichéd. Let's try . . .

Those cool eyes gazed down at him, calming
like the green of

It needed something different, something fresh,
something outside of myself --
*Sifting through my recollections, coming to me in just
this order, in just this way:*

- the green of a mossy lake with turtles bobbing their heads in and out
    verdant grass of a treeless green meadow
        moist lime, its juices flowing through its skin
            lush leaves swaying in the breeze
                a green sash wrapped about the waist of an Irish lassie
                a shimmering tray of jade

Green. The sense of it clamped onto my mind. It wasn't going
away. My mother in a green bathing suit. Turning her head toward
the person watching her. Smiling. Younger than I had ever known
her to be. It was another's thought, another's vision.

I looked in my pocket appointment book. This evening I was
going to a bookstore in the Upper East Side for a reading and signing
of Evolved Parameters. I would be meeting my literary agent there.
Something to look forward to. Except . . .

A hunch. Or a precognitive insight. Or a sudden phobic irrationality.

Tonight's event would be open to the public. It had been widely
advertised. Anyone could come. Anyone like that stranger who saved
me from those teenaged muggers a week ago. Or that mustached
little man in the subway who held that vision of Mom in his head.
One, or both. Or, perhaps . . .

I drew in a deep shaky breath.

Tonight I might very well meet Mr. Quiver.

CHAPTER ELEVEN
A Book Signing

I was on another planet fighting for breath. My chest heaved as I rapidly sucked in air, losing my footing all the while. I fought for control in a losing battle as the terrain closed in upon me. I grappled with its rounded mountains, my head lolling in the dangerous caress of its rolling valley. Pressed against its surface, I listened to the tumultuous heartbeat of the world. Dazed, I stared up at two glittering suns beating down upon me in their merciless glare. Wisps of golden filaments whipped over my face. I felt as if I were melting into that expanse. Inevitably I became part of the planet called Tracy Lessing.

"Don't . . ." Tracy moaned, grabbing my forearm and pressing my hand against the globes of her breasts. I knew she meant 'Don't stop.' Her lips on mine were moist, her tongue darting past my teeth to touch the walls of my mouth. Tingling, enraptured, I let her probe, my eyes gazing into hers.

Two nudes on a plush white rug. Tracy's thought. *A hearth with an orange-glowing fireplace behind them warmed the unclothed man and woman as they rolled in embrace, bodies dripping with effort.*

She had eyes the color of thunder clouds, storm-filled and longing. Great strands of shoulder-length hair fell over my eyes, hair of reddish gold like the sun-stippled sky at dawn. Her perfumed hair, the fragrance of fresh roses, surrounded me. Her mutable eyes burned deeply into me.

Tracy cried out and shook, her hips lunging against me. *Muscle touching flesh, flesh upon flesh, two eager bodies entwined.*

I felt the heat rising to my face as I watched the two denuded figures clasping one another in Tracy's imagination, alive with lust -- and her thoughts became mine.

I was cradled in her arm and Planet Tracy let her fine fingers stroke the back of my neck, lulling me into a pleasantly erotic drowse. With her other hand, she grasped my wrists and directed them under her sheer blouse, guiding me as if I were a little boy, allowing me – no, urging me – to explore her great nipples and those delight-stirring breasts trembling under my touch. She was responsive entirely to my contact. Fingers upon flesh, I was joined to her, magnetized and clinging.

She moaned, her leg shifting between mine. I shivered and felt my body shatter. I struggled to block the moist discharge from breaking.

A door clanged open and footsteps clashed against metal on the staircase. Somewhere above, voices: "Down this way," "I thought they went . . ." "Mr. Brocton?"

The world slipped away and left me in a cement-walled staircase. Footsteps from above rushed closer, shadows splashed against the walls. Excited voices echoed vaguely.

Tracy Lessing buttoned her soft green blouse, already having slipped on her navy-blue business jacket. With a shake of her disheveled hair and the smoothing of her blue navy knee-length dress, she was suddenly the well-ordered professional executive. I brushed my fallen locks out of my eyes, my shirt hanging out of my corduroys, and stared at her in amazement.

"How? . . ." I began.

She clamped stolid hands over my mouth. "Put your jacket on," she whispered. "Pick that up."

I stared down at the stairs. My book was laying there, folded notes for my reading sticking out of it. I grabbed up my tweed jacket from the metal rail where I had shoved it, clumsily pulled it over my shoulders and thrust my arms into the sleeves. It was my favorite tweed, a light brown jacket with leather patches on the elbows. Everyone expects a great writer to wear one at a reading. I had three.

"Hurry the hell up!" Tracy whispered hoarsely.

I grabbed up my book and raced to button my shirt while pushing the shirttails into my pants. No doubt I looked awkward in the extreme when two men found us. I hoped I simply looked eccentric and wistful.

"Mr. Brocton! There you are!" The voice came from a fiftyish man who was in charge of the speaker program of the national chain of Levinson's Book Sellers. He lowered his half-rimmed spectacles to scrutinize me.

"Yes, Mr. Speakman. Here I am."

Mr. Martin Speakman was remarkable in having a name so appropriately suited to his job description. I had dealt with him three or four times in the past, both here in New York and in Philadelphia. Just now as I looked up the staircase at him, I read his thoughts of his unattractive wife and three buck-toothed little daughters. He was devoted to them. He glared at me with disapproval, recognizing the proximity between myself and my literary agent on the stairs as sexual attentiveness. I found him utterly boring.

"We were concerned when we couldn't find you, Alex," said the second man, Jeremy Winters, one of the assistant managers at the Fourteenth Street bookstore in whose staircase we loitered. "Everything all right?"

At six foot four, Jeremy towered over Mr. Speakman, Tracy, and myself. An amiable fellow with a long face, steady blue eyes, and a ready smile, Jeremy was a huge fan of science fiction. We talked often when I was in Levinson's about my novels, a topic I usually encouraged, and he told me what he liked and disliked in them. He rarely if ever flattered me. I liked him a lot.

"We're good," Tracy answered. "We were conferring over Alex's deadline for the new book."

Tracy Lessing was so deadpan in her delivery that I was about to crack up. Craning my neck up at Jeremy though, I saw his idyllic image of her as a small and vulnerable beauty. I very nearly doubled over then and there with laughter. To young Jeremy, Ms. Lessing was unapproachable; a creature of such exquisiteness that he held her with deep and abiding respect. I recognized that image immediately as puppy love. In light of knowing Jeremy's feelings for Planet Tracy, I restrained my frivolous response despite my just having explored in her a great deal more than 'puppy' love.

I looked steadily up at Mr. Speakman and Jeremy, and kept my voice low: "I find Ms. Lessing's decisions most stringent." A subtle burst of exhalation escaped my lips. "But I'm sure we can reach some sort of reconciliation." I held the men's eyes in a long pause. "Soon."

Tracy gave me a sidelong look and turned back to them. "Shall we go? How is the turnout?"

"Real good," said Jeremy. "You've drawn a large crowd, Alex. I had to set up a couple of more rows of chairs."

Mr. Speakman led us upstairs and into the upper floor. Numbers of people sat in rows, every chair taken, talking quietly to each other. They faced a podium with an empty chair beside it. On the wall behind the podium was the embossed lettering of "Levinson's Booksellers." Several people stood restively behind the last row.

"There's Alex Brocton," cried a middle-aged woman standing nearest to the stairway door. I gave her a grin and nodded as I strode past her toward the podium. I took the chair facing the audience and casually crossed my legs.

Mr. Speakman had kept up with me and headed directly to the podium. I noted Planet Tracy leaning sensuously against the 'Crafts' bookcase, eyeing a gray-haired, dignified gentleman standing to her right. I noticed he noticed her. She noticed that, too.

Jeremy stayed inconspicuously conspicuous in the back, all the while watching Tracy. I resisted the urge to wave to Jeremy and call out: "Over here, Jeremy!"

While Speakman gave a brief, highly laudatory introduction, I looked through my copy of Evolved Parameters and fingered the pages where I would begin my reading. I was trying to affect an air of humility as Speakman spoke my praises.

A pause from Speakman. I saw him move his head left and right as he scanned the audience. I knew what was coming. It was my cue.

"And now . . . Alex Brocton!"

I rose and enjoyed the applause as I smoothly went up to Speakman, shook his hand, and released it. He stepped aside and sat while I bowed with simple grace to the crowd. I had become quite practiced in all this.

"Thank you. Thank you." People gradually halted their clapping. "I want to thank Mr. Martin Speakman for arranging this engagement." More applause. An 'engagement' made this sound rather like a glamorous social occasion. At any rate, I wanted the audience to feel that way.

"Those of you who have been reading the cover blurb of my novel may have figured out the premise of Evolved Parameters. Life, our experience of life, is filled with complexity. Of course that must be so. In the same way, I try to show the complexity of life in my novels and Evolved Parameters is no exception. I have several major characters interconnecting with one another. The point of the novel is that as people evolve, their relationships change."

"Isn't that always true?" called out a young blonde-haired man in the second row. "I mean, isn't it ordinary for people's relationships to change over time?"

"Yes," I answered. "Usually that's what happens. But my book takes it a bit further. Sometimes that evolution is formed by means outside, by forces that we have no control over. In the novel, something sinister, something inexplicable, is creating a sudden burst in human evolution. Initially, those – parameters – appear to be wondrous. But they quickly become dangerous, even fatal, to all of humanity. That, very simply, is the theme of the work before you. Simple. And complex."

"Let me read to you from an early chapter," I continued. "It's when Jennifer Farrell notices the physical change in herself. She's getting ready for the party, sitting at her bedroom mirror."

All the while, my eyes scanned the audience. *Is Mr. Quiver here? Is it my cousin Howard? Or could Mr. Quiver be the tall beady-eyed man who was that childhood bully who strangled me? I don't see either of them here . . .*

I opened a bottle of water that sat on the podium and drank. I relished the silence in the room. After I put the bottle down, I took a breath and said, "Well, here goes."

I read the better part of a chapter. The crowd before me was silent with excitement. Later, when a line formed and I sat behind a table signing autographs, I babbled banalities that meant nothing. But fans of my work smiled and babbled on as I signed whatever silly remark they asked me to add onto the title page.

"Hello! Alex Brocton."

I looked up at the slender young man who stood holding my novel in a clenched hand. It was the same fellow who had called out during my speech calling my premise about changing relationships 'ordinary' -- his words. He smiled in a disarming way. He was clearly younger than me, maybe twenty years old. Dressed in a blue sweater, gray trousers, and white striped, open-necked shirt, he was male-model handsome; slicked-back blonde hair, high cheek bones, straight nose, white teeth, blue-gray sparkling eyes.

"Do I know you?" I asked, knowing that I didn't know him at all.

"I wish," he answered with a chuckle. He had a boyish charm about him. "I'm thrilled to finally meet you, Alex."

I took a moment to glance around and saw that Tracy and the dignified gentleman were nowhere to be seen. However, Mr. Speakman and Jeremy were talking quietly off to one side of the autograph line.

I turned back to the young man who was holding my book tightly, not giving it up. "Would you like me to sign that?"

"Absolutely." He shifted his shoulders as he handed me the book. He had been carrying a large manila envelope under his arm and transferred it to his other hand.

I found the title page of the book and poised my marking pen. "Who should I make it out to?"

He rubbed his perfect chin and said, "Dylan Lance."

"Sounds like an actor's name." I leaned into the page as I signed it. "That really your name?"

"No." He took back his book and looked behind him. Five more people in line. With a smile, he stepped aside to let them come ahead. Dylan Lance stayed near as I spoke to the remaining people and finished signing.

For a moment, he and I stared at each other in awkward silence. In the time since we had talked, I had become used to his presence. He held me in his mind, registering my movements and expressions as I spoke to the others.

Before I finished signing, Speakman and Jeremy had waved and walked away to take care of other duties. I knew that Jeremy would soon return to put away the extra copies of <u>Evolved Parameters</u> that hadn't been purchased.

"Well," I said, "you were saying something about your name. Dylan Lance a stage name?"

"No, Alex. It's a pen name. I'm trying to break into writing."

Oh shit! "Well, Dylan Lance may be a little . . . sharp. For a writer's pen name. What's your real name?"

He suddenly turned into a gawky little boy. "Uh, it's . . . Dennis Leibowitz. See? Wouldn't exactly inspire readers, would it?"

"Oh, I don't know. It sounds quite literary, actually."

He thrust out the manila envelope. "I brought this for you, Alex."

Shit! Shit! Shit!

"I'd like you to read it."

Get me the hell out of here!

"It's a terrific science fiction novel I'm writing."

Give me a gun, somebody! Let me finish him off quick.

"You can write on it. Make any corrections you need to. I've got copies."

A machete! Get me a machete! I'll slice him to pieces along with his novel!

"Would you take a look at it, Alex?"

I gazed into his blue-gray eyes that began to water over and gulped. "Dennis –"

"Dylan."

"Dylan --" *I'll use my bare hands! Strangle the S.O.B.* "I'm a writer. I don't do that kind of thing. You need a good editor. Pay somebody. Don't take it to a friend. Try going online and finding a critique group. Okay?"

Too abrupt. Too blunt. I know. But in a case like this, you gotta rip the bandage off in one move!

"Would it hurt if you just took a look?" His eyes were pleading now. "Just read the first page. Tell me what you think."

"It won't do any good, Dylan. I can't tell you from a single page. Not in two minutes or two hours or two weeks. I'm simply not into doing that kind of thing. I'm sure you can see that." I was sure that he couldn't.

The forced smile on his face died. His watery eyes dried suddenly. He pulled the envelope back and slapped it under his arm. He held out his signed copy of my book, spine toward me. "Thanks, MISTER Brocton. For signing my book."

He turned, went to the escalator, and started down, never looking back at me.

But I saw what he was thinking. I saw things through *his* mind and I knew it was how he saw me. I was sitting at this table, looking slightly upward, my face showing a cryptic Mona Lisa smile. In his thoughts, my eyes transformed into a hard cold stare; my lips twisted down with scorn. His view of me was becoming increasingly unflattering.

To him, I was an arrogant bastard. Even after he descended from view, I felt the heat of his hatred.

I sensed his emotions so intensely that they stayed with me. I couldn't shake them as readily as I could images coming from others. The hairs stood up at the back of my neck. They were HIS feelings. But they blended with my own, fighting for dominance. Which sensations were mine and which were his? I was in a cold sweat.

As I closed my copy of Evolved Parameters, I realized this young man, Dennis, had left me with a different sensation. I had miss-identified it as hatred. That wasn't it. It took a moment. Suddenly, I knew: *desperation!*

CHAPTER TWELVE
PhenomenomiCon, PA

"**A**lex!" Skye Carrigan, Ambassador of the Congrevian Star System shouted from across the crowded ballroom. I saw what was in her mind: me, brown-haired, tall, sharp-eyed behind my eyeglasses, chiseled chin (an ideal version, certainly). She sped toward me, her yellow and green Congreve uniform gleaming with rhinestones as she plowed past people. "Alex! Wait!"

I wasn't going anywhere. I had been heading for an empty table with my drink in hand when Skye caught my attention. She was blonde and bulging in her costume. She was also five foot nothing and weighed two hundred pounds. A true fan.

"I'm so glad I saw you," she said breathlessly. "You remember me, don't you?"

"You look very familiar," I said. *Not at all.* "Could you have been at Lasercon?"

"That's right!" She thrust the spine of a book into my face. "Sign this for me, Alex?"

I edged toward a nearby table that was occupied by a flock of truefen (plural form of dedicated SF fans. In this particular instance, these truefen consisted of three adolescent boys and one green-haired female). The four of them stared curiously up at me. Only one of them, a scarecrow-thin boy, had a thought. He was imagining the green-haired girl in bed with him, naked.

I slipped my drink onto the edge of the table and reached for Skye's book. It was one of my older novels, something called Slipstream Season. I saw that it was a first edition. I also saw it had a large coffee stain on the first four pages. And it had a mark-down label covering the $30.00 price on the dust jacket, ink-marked at $5.00. Skye had probably just purchased it in the dealer's room.

"Who should I make it out to?" I asked and brought out a felt-tipped pen from my second-favorite tweed jacket.

"Make it out to me!"

I took a beat as I gaped at her. I thought about writing "To Me." I wrote: "To Gladys—Imagine a whole world; then just live it! – Alex Brocton"

Skye grabbed the book and read my inscription. "You *do* remember me, Alex!"

"Certainly, Gladys. How could I ever forget you?"

Skye squealed, touched my arm, and waddled off to join a rotund kid dressed as Captain Asteroid.

How did I know Ambassador Skye's real name? You really want to know? Everyone who registers for a science fiction convention wears a name badge. Hers was on her yellow utility belt.

I smiled at the truefen at the table and picked up my drink. I fled before they could possibly have a clue who I was. If they read books at all.

Friday night. Meet the Pros Party. This was where truefen and professional writers rubbed elbows. Free liquor for the pros. We were given cash bar tickets. The fen had to pay their own way. For the next hour or two, depending on how visible I remained, I was available for discussion with anyone in the room. Fortunately, I had my free cash bar ticket. So . . . I circulated, drink in hand.

"Hey! Alex! Been a while, hasn't it?" came a voice from my left. Winding through the crowd was the editor of *Incredible Stories Magazine*, Nicholas Giancola. He came at me dressed in a navy blue suit, patent-leather shoes, striped shirt, and, traditionally, no tie. Nick never wore a tie. He hated them. About forty-five years old, he had been a boy wonder, a renowned 'zine founder and editor while still in his twenties. He was four inches taller than me and pot-bellied. And he never shaved close to his face; he had a perpetual two-day growth of whiskers.

"How you've been, Alex?" He slapped me on the shoulder so hard that my eyeglasses joggled above my nose and I had to grab them. His mind swirled with multi-images: darts tossed at the face of his ex-wife, a giant serpent wrapping itself around a bikini-clad blonde, taking cash out of an ATM, and punching out Captain America – the comic-book version. Other things, less defined, swam in his head. I knew he wanted something from me.

"Feeling good," I said, setting my glasses back on. "How 'bout you?"

"Been wondering, Alex." He leaned into me and gazed down at my drink. "You have another cash bar ticket? Can't find mine."

"No. Sorry, Nick. I used my last one. What's up?"

"I'm putting together an anthology of weird shapeshifter stories for *Final Journey Press*. Didn't you say back in January you were working on a story like that?"

"Yeah, Nick, I did. You rejected it in March."

"I did? What was it? Was it the family of werebears piece? What was it again?"

"That's right. They were actual bears that were cursed to spend their daylight hours as humans. I called it "A Bear We All Have to Cross." You emailed me the shortest rejection I ever received: "Not for us.""

"Well, I'm rethinking that now. I'd like --"

Totally unexpectedly, I was grabbed from behind. Strong arms grasped me around my upper shoulders and held me solidly around the neck. Nick sputtered in shock as I dropped my drink over his nice blue suit.

I should've detected the movement beforehand. Whoever it was, he was able to block any thoughts. And I mean, completely block me out.

I called out, "What's going on?" I fought to get my breath.

"Got you, you son of a bitch!" That's when I realized it was a girl. A particularly strong girl. The voice was disguised but I thought I knew it. I also caught a whiff of a familiar perfume.

"Let . . . go." I tried to pull away but she also wrapped her ankles around my calves. "What do you think --"

Nick shouted, "I'd better go for help." He stood there, looking wildly around at the people gathering closer and watching in awe.

Four large Armorean Swamp warriors in full battle regalia were pushing their way toward us. I struggled to break the girl's handhold, stumbling around while onlookers backed off.

Nearly toppling into a table, I held onto it as I steadied myself. The girl's unshakeable grip tightened around my neck. I felt icy sweat sliding down my back.

I was quite certain that in one quick move, the girl would snap my neck.

CHAPTER THIRTEEN
A Short Drive Away

I felt the pulse of my carotids quickening with the tightness of the girl's arm around my throat. I drew in quick breaths as sweat slid down my shirt. My glasses had misted as I glared at Nick Giancola who looked back helplessly.

The four Armorean Swamp warriors reached us and started pulling at the girl's arms. She yelled fiercely and I felt her grip loosening. Several things came to my mind all at once: The girl had deliberately avoided knocking off my glasses when she grabbed me; she had purposely prevented my reading her thoughts – as if she knew about my ability; and, I had known this girl pretty much my whole life.

By then, one of the costumed Armoreans, the oldest and hoariest of the four, held the girl by her wrist and I saw who she was. In his deep guttural voice, the grizzled Armorean said, "We'll escort her out. Let's go."

"No you don't!" The girl pulled out of his grip. To me: "Tell him it's okay."

I raised my hands in the universal sign for LET'S ALL CALM DOWN NOW!

"It's okay," I called out. "She was just kidding around. No one's hurt. Okay?"

The Armoreans looked at each other. They weren't official guards or anything. They were volunteers for the Con committee.

"Okay," said the gray-haired Armorean who had held the girl. "But the Con frowns on this kind of 'kidding around.' Has anybody been hurt?"

"Me," answered Nick. "My jacket. This famous author spilled his damn drink all over it."

I leaned toward him and whispered, "Shut up, Nick. I'll pay for it."

"Here," the girl leapt toward Nick. "Here's ten bucks. That's more than cleaning your suit's worth, I'm willing to bet."

"Maybe." Glowering at her, Nick pocketed the cash.

The Armorean warrior shouted, "Show's over!" People casually meandered away, laughing and talking and sipping their drinks. The four Armoreans grunted at each other, mainly for appearance sake, and strode away.

Nick looked the girl over and turned to me. "Who is this young lady?"

She had started going through her belt pouch when Nick spoke. She looked up at him and smiled a bright lovely smile, her eyes sparkling with feigned interest. Unkempt dark hair fell over her eyes and she brushed it away. She wore a dark brown pants suit made for roughing it. I knew her to be more of a tomboy than a 'young lady,' but she suddenly acted sweet innocence for Nick.

"Go ahead, tell him. Tell him, Alexander Patrick."

She walked up to Nick and put a firm hand on his shoulder. She was a few inches shorter than me, so Nick towered over her. But she was in total control. Nick smiled broadly. "Who ARE you?" he asked. He turned to me. "Your middle name is Patrick?"

I ignored him, choosing to play host. "Nicholas Giancola, publishing giant --" I gestured with a sweep of my arm – "this is Alyson Brocton. My sister."

"Alyson Brocton *Gainer*, actually," she said. "I'm married. Remember?"

Nick's eyes widened. He turned again to me. "I didn't know you had a sister."

"You don't know a lot of things about me."

He turned back to Aly. "Would you like to join me at the hotel bar for a drink?" Nick seemed not to have heard the 'I'm married' part. Or didn't care.

I could see Aly's distaste and sensed her applying pressure to her grip on Nick's shoulder. Aly was not a subtle person.

"Some other time, Nick," she said. "I need some private time with my brother."

Nick squirmed under Aly's tight hold. He pulled away and gave a wry smile. "Another time," he replied. He blended quickly into the crowded room.

Aly came to me and gave a peck on my cheek.

"It's quite a surprise to see you here," I told her. "What brings you to the Con?"

"Brian's playing in a bridge tournament in Cherry Hill." I knew Brian. Aly's husband. "I saw on your website that you would be at this Philly convention, so I decided to drive over. I need to talk to you. Let's go take a walk outside."

We headed into the lobby and crossed to the sliding doors.

Aly might know about Uncle George. Sure. Of course! She was closer to Mom than to Dad, and Mom might have talked to her about Uncle George's hand shadows. Maybe Mom even told her about 'Mr. Quiver.' Aly talked to Mom a lot in her teenage years. Yeah. Mr. Quiver! Got to ask Aly what she knows about that!

"So," Aly said, "you didn't know it was me when I jumped you?" She stared at me with disconcerting intensity. This wasn't a casual question.

"No, I didn't. You blocked me out, as usual. Didn't you?"

"I don't even think about it," she said, and smiled. "I know you so well."

Outside the hotel, we strolled down a walkway, headed for the street. It was a still night and clear. We could see the stars over us.

"I'm glad you're here," I said. "I wanted to ask you --"

"I need you to tell me!" she interrupted. "You *really* didn't sense who I was? I mean, you couldn't see my feelings? You couldn't tell I was there – that it was me?"

Why was she harping on that? "I told you. No."

"Then . . . then you weren't changed after the car accident? Like when you went blind from that killer's gun blast that summer in Monticello? I thought maybe the accident would have increased your – whatever it is – you know what I'm talking about!"

Why's she bringing that up? She hadn't asked me about my special ability in the past. She didn't want to know anything about it before.

"No." I tried for a grin. I could talk freely. This was my sister, after all. "I'm still the same old snoopy mind reader I always was. Reading people I get to know. Except you. I don't think that's changed in any way." Aly looked away, pensive. *What was she thinking?* I still couldn't read her. She doesn't let me.

"I've been thinking about the car accident a lot lately." Her voice choked up. "I've been thinking about Mom." She turned to me. "Did the accident change you in any way? You don't talk about it."

No, I don't talk about it. It happened four years ago. Mom was driving me to the airport. We had been celebrating at their old house in Whitestone. Mom and Dad and Aly and her husband Brian and me. I was getting an award for my latest brilliant novel back then. Anyway, Aly and Brian left early. Bri had a morning math class at the community college where he taught. Dad had worked all day and was dead on his feet. So Mom volunteered to drive me to La Guardia. It was only a five minute drive.

"I don't remember much about it, Aly. I can't tell if anything changed in me."

I was going to a WorldCon in San Antonio. My flight was at ten. I didn't remember what happened. Next thing I knew, I was in the hospital and bandaged and itchy from burns on my body and that's all I knew.

Stop now. I don't want to think about it. Go to something else. Please!

"What were you and Mom talking about in the car?"

Hell, just stop! Why do you have to bring that whole thing up?

I only knew that Mom died in the crash. And afterward, the doctors told me I had died, too. But they brought me back. Reborn.

The doctors told me I was very lucky. I wasn't feeling lucky at all. Just pain. And itching.

I tried to remember Mom's face. I mean now, in the present, standing with Aly outside the hotel in Philadelphia. I couldn't do it. I couldn't picture my mother.

"Do you think about her much?" Aly asked.

"Yes. Yes, I do." Now I could bring it up. I told Larry Coates about what happened a week ago. The two teen psychos and Mr. Quiver. I could surely tell Aly. "Do you remember Mom's Uncle George?"

Aly looked at me as if she had been shaken awake. "What? Uncle George? What's that old fart got to do with anything?"

"Do you remember he could form shadow figures with his hands?"

"Alex, what are you talking about?"

"You know. Hand shadows on the wall. Mom ever talk about him? She say anything about 'Mr. Quiver?'"

"Mr. Quiver? I'm talking about Mom! About what you were saying to her! The car accident! You're deliberately changing the subject. I want to know what you said to her in the car before the crash. Well?"

"Why's that important? I can't remember what we talked about. How could I?"

"Did you tell her you could see into her thoughts?"

"What? No." I was bewildered and unnerved. Why was Aly asking that? "I don't know. I don't remember anything about that. Look, two people have approached me. I got a note saying that I'm being watched. It was signed 'Mr. Quiver.' Dad told me that name came from Uncle George --"

"Uncle George is dead."

"I know. But Cousin Howard is alive. I think he's one of the men who approached me. He talked to me in the subway."

"You said there were two."

"Yeah. The other's a big guy. He helped me when a couple of teenagers were trying to mug me. I think years ago he was a boy who strangled me when I was a three-year old. Do you know anything more about Howard? Anything?"

"It's been years since I've seen Howard. I barely knew Uncle George. Never heard of Mr. Quiver either." She touched my arm. "Did they try to hurt you, these two?"

"No. But I don't like the idea that they're watching me. They know – about me."

She stepped away and looked up at the night sky. "Wish I could tell you something useful. And here I've been badgering you about Mom. You really don't remember if you scared her before the accident?"

"Scared her? What do you mean?"

"Scared her! Told her things she was thinking! She knew there was something special about you. But she didn't know what it was. It never occurred to her that you could read her mind. She talked to me about you, concerned about the way you acted. Like you knew things children don't usually know. You didn't tell her, did you, Alex?"

"No! Of course not."

"You didn't tell her something in the car? Something only she would know?"

"No, Aly! I didn't. I wouldn't."

"Did you tell her something intimate? Something nobody else was supposed to know? Did you?

"Absolutely not!"

"Tell me the truth!"

"I'm telling you."

"DID YOU CAUSE HER TO CRASH THE CAR?"

CHAPTER FOURTEEN
Afterimage

I stared at Aly, dumbstruck. Her eyes flared at me, lips twisted with anger. For the briefest of moments, I saw Mom's face in Aly's features. I trembled under her scrutiny.

"Well?" she said, her voice softening with calm. "Did you? Say anything to upset Mom?"

"I wouldn't tell her anything that would upset her. Aly, come on! If we talked in the car, it was likely about my flight. I don't really remember. I probably talked about the award I was getting. The other authors who would be there. I'm only guessing at that. I don't have any memory of the accident at all."

Slowly, Aly came close to me and whispered, "Mom was secretly seeing a man."

I was completely taken aback. I knew about her lover, of course. After all, I had decided that the big guy with far apart eyes who saved me from the mugging a week ago was the son of Mom's lover. The same boy who strangled me when I was three years old.

But how did Aly know Mom had a lover?

"How do you know that?" I asked softly.

"Mom told me." Aly grabbed my shoulder, turned me toward the hotel, and led me back, holding onto my arm in a sign of affection that we seldom showed one another. "Mom talked to me about a lot of things that she couldn't talk about with anyone else. She had to tell *someone*. She *had* to." Aly stopped walking. She reached up and lightly brushed my hair. I was stunned by the unaccustomed action. "Did you know she was seeing another man? Did you see that in her mind?"

The world suddenly stopped. It was a moment frozen in time. Aly waited.

"No, Aly. I didn't."

She pressed her lips together and turned away, striding back to the hotel entrance. I rushed to catch up. For an instant, she let her defenses down and revealed what she was thinking. It was the first time in memory.

Aly saw herself sitting on the bed in our parents' room, Mom next to her. It was that night. The night we were celebrating. Before Mom drove me to the airport.

How did I know all that? The when of it? Somehow that gets communicated to me when I see someone's thoughts.

Mom's eyes were misty as she talked to Aly in the bedroom. It was all from Aly's perspective. Aly silently gauged Mom's gestures, memorized her eyes and lips and short brown hair, attentive to her voice. Mom looked so much like Aly.

"Ohhhh!" A loud exclamation. Mom. In reading thoughts, I don't hear voices. There is no comic-book bubble above people's faces where I see words. But, since the accident four years ago, I occasionally hear sounds, especially when they're important to the person thinking them. Natural sounds mostly. Running water, the sizzle of meat cooking, whistles and hums and clanging. And once in a great while, I can hear the sound of anger or exasperation or crying in a person's mind, while seeing what he or she sees.

"Walk me downstairs to my car," Aly said and clasped my hand.

I saw Nick Giancola walking toward us in the lobby. He spotted me and was about to approach. He saw Aly beside me then and thought better of it. He turned away and called out to someone, then headed away.

At the elevators, Aly pressed the down button. We waited.

"You don't hear the words, do you?" she said, staring straight ahead.

"What do you mean?"

"When you see someone's thoughts, you can't hear what is said."

She had purposely let me see what she was thinking! "No, I can't." *She's not going to shake me up with her damned intuitive cleverness. I am a rock.*

One of the elevator doors opened and we went in. Aly pressed the button for lower level – parking.

"Mom was telling me," here Aly seemed to choke on her words, "how much she loved us. You and me. She was saying, how much she would miss us . . ."

"What? Aly. What is it?"

The elevator doors opened. Three teenaged girls and two boys stood there and let us squeeze by before they piled in.

Aly held on to my arm and pulled me along, none too gently. She walked fast, seeking her car.

"Maybe you don't know," she said. "Maybe she kept it so hidden that she wouldn't even think about it." Aly looked sharply at me. "Especially around you. Not that she knew you could read her mind. But, still, she would keep that closed from everybody. Even you. Somehow."

We reached Aly's car, a compact Dodge in green and gold. She beeped the doors unlocked and opened the driver's side door. "She wanted to tell me," she said, looking at me. "That night. She almost did. I think she was just about to when Dad walked in on us."

"Almost told you what?"

Aly looked away momentarily, then turned her gaze fully on me. "I've thought about it. It's just a guess. I saw something in the way Mom talked to Dad when he interrupted us. Yes. I think I'm right."

"What is it?"

"I think Mom was planning to go away. I think she was leaving us."

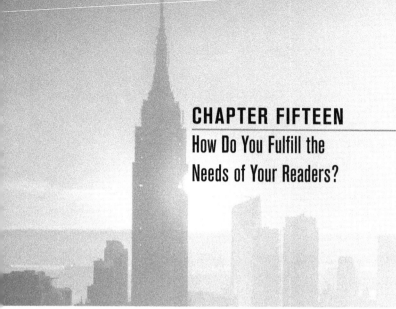

CHAPTER FIFTEEN
How Do You Fulfill the Needs of Your Readers?

Mom leaving us? Was Aly right about that?

Mom's eyes water as she gives a soft cry. She takes Aly's hand in hers and caresses her cheek . . .

I still saw Aly's thoughts of Mom even after she had driven through the underground garage and was nowhere in sight. It was an afterimage. *Mom sitting on the bed that last night. Before the car accident.*

But did I actually see what Aly was thinking? Couldn't it simply have been my imagination recreating those things that Aly revealed as we spoke?

No. I still see Aly's thought. I know it. She may be a mile away by now, but I continue to see her thinking. Our connection is that strong. Afterimages.

Were you really going to leave us, Mom? Where would you have gone? With HIM? Were you --

I looked at my watch.

"Shit!" I had a panel. Already started. Twelve minutes ago!

I sped across the lobby to the staircase and stormed up the steps, two at a time . . .

"That's why I believe the best story-telling is myth-making," said the straw-haired fortyish woman in the drab green dress seated on the platform. "Readers want to read fiction that has enduring meaning and that's why we, as authors, should be striving to create myths."

Next to the woman, a tanned man in an immaculate blue suit and with a pure-white mane of hair said, "I agree with you, Jocelyn, to *this* degree. It's less important that writers consciously attempt to create myth when . . ."

It was ten-seventeen, Friday night. The panel topic was "How Do You Fulfill the Needs of Your Readers." I rushed onto the platform with mumbled apologies and squeezed into an empty chair between the two speakers. All of us on the panel were novelists. Some of us were world famous.

Not me. At least, not yet. But Dr. Fennaday at my right elbow, the deeply-tanned, white-maned gentleman – he was a living legend. Not many of them left.

Before us was an audience of, I'd say, about thirty people. Four of us sat on the panel. I had placed myself between Jocelyn Wynmore, the author of the SturmScar Battalion series, and Dominick Fennaday, the Nobel-prize winning physicist and legendary writer of the classic science fiction novel The TeleKorax Domain. On the other side of Dr. Fennaday was the prolific Black author of numerous novels and short stories, Byron Knowles. He was the moderator of the panel.

Dr. Fennaday leaned toward me, his piercing blue eyes ablaze, and whispered, "Mr. Brocton, I must talk to you after the panel."

Dominick Fennaday MUST talk to me! I stared at him with open astonishment. Before I could reply, Knowles addressed the audience.

"As you can see, the final member of our panel has joined us. Alex, would you introduce yourself?"

"Thank you, Byron. My name is Alex Brocton. I've done a little writing." That got a laugh. "Sorry I'm so late. I was in the bar arm-wrestling with my book editor. I think he beat me. I won't know for sure until I get my next check." Some more laughs. Then I gave a brief precis of my published novels, some of which received a smattering of applause from the audience.

"Okay, Alex," said Byron. "We were just getting into what writers do to involve readers in our stories. What's your take on that?"

"That's a large question," I said, still trying to wrap my head around the topic. I tried to sense what my fellow panelists were thinking but I couldn't read any of them. Not yet, anyway. It takes more familiarity with others before I can actually get a sense of how they're feeling and then be able to delve into thoughts. And, I should tell you, sometimes I can't read people at all. I don't really have control over everything I do.

So, I focused on the thirty or so people in front of me and plunged in. "When I work on a novel, I write to please myself, first and foremost. That's not to say I ignore my readers. But I aim my writing toward someone on the same level as me. Someone who likes the same sort of things that I do. When I read anyone else's fiction, what I enjoy most is when a story takes me by surprise. And then, carries me along with its journey of discovery.

"So, I write with the intention of creating the same kind of reaction in my readers."

I heard the ring tones of "Funeral March of a Marionette" close by and knew it was my own cell phone. I quickly pulled it out of my jacket pocket, saw the caller ID, and answered it.

"I can't talk now," I said, more harshly than I intended.

"This is Larry," the familiar voice said. "Larry Coates."

"I know," I answered. "I have to call you back."

"This is important, Alex. I've got good news."

"You've caught me in the middle of a panel. And *I'm* the one who's talking!"

"How much time till your panel ends?"

I gestured to the audience that I would be just a moment longer. "I'll get back to you in twenty minutes." I felt the heat of Dominick Fennaday's shoulder and turned to him. His sharp eyes ploughed into my soul. Returning to my phone, I said, "Thirty-five minutes, Larry. Okay?"

"I'll call *you* back, Alex. I'm not in my office. You'll be surprised where I am."

"Oh? Where are you?"

"I'm with your cousin Howard in New Jersey. You know. Mr. Quiver?"

CHAPTER SIXTEEN
Will the Real Mister Quiver Please Stand Up?

"**A**s I see it, Alex, your Gssynnic Archive novels discard the notion of travel through hyperspace as physically impossible," Dom Fennaday said, his eyes bright with fervor. "That alien perspective of using somatic wave transference is so compelling to me. Utterly preposterous! But the theory is told with such a unique point of view that it sounds nearly probable. Letting the reader see your variant physics through the eyes of Lell, a member of the Gssynn race, was a clever tact on your part."

I sat back on the cushioned chair and smiled. "Thank you, Dom. I feel honored hearing you say that."

He insisted I call him Dom. I'm talking about the legendary physicist and speculative fiction novelist (He doesn't call his novels science fiction), Dr. Dominick Jeremy Fennaday. Here he was, as real as anyone, sitting inches from me! Blue eyes sparkling, his mane of white hair shimmering, chuckling with me and reveling in my writing, alternately querying and praising. My life had reached its zenith.

We sat in a quiet corner of the hotel lobby where Dr. Fennaday hadn't yet been discovered by his legion of fans. Even at eleven o'clock at night, there were still numbers of people meandering around. A few, young and middle-aged, sat in comfortable chairs and soft-cushioned sofas around us, talking to one another.

"Tell me," Dom said and leaned forward with enthusiasm. "When are you getting back to Gssynn? It's been too many years since your last book in the series."

"Well, I think it'll be soon." I resisted calling him 'Dom' again. I didn't want to seem too fawning. "I'm working on a new novel right now, but, after that's finished, I expect I'll return --"

'Funeral March of a Marionette' played on my cell phone. A quick check of my watch showed that I'd spent only twenty-five minutes with Dr. Fennaday. Granted, I could have spent hours talking to the prize-winning novelist, I had hoped for fifteen minutes more, at least. No name on the caller ID. I didn't recognize the phone number.

"Excuse me," I told the Good Doctor. "This'll just take a minute." Into the phone: "I was going to call you back on your cell, Larry! Where are you?"

"362 Evergreen Lane, Metuchen, New Jersey."

"Larry?"

"This is Howard. Your cousin, Howard Schuyler. Mr. Coates is here with me. I have you on speaker so he can listen, too."

I turned back to Dom but a trio of comely young women stood over Dr. Fennaday and were talking to him. The Good Doctor beamed at me and gave a wink, got up, and allowed himself to be pulled away.

I mouthed a 'good-bye' and saw that it was largely ignored. I sat alone, feeling a bit dejected in my little corner of the world.

I practically hit myself in the mouth with my cell phone. "Hello? Howard? I have some questions for you."

"I bet you have!" He laughed a good hardy laugh. His voice was a full-throated baritone, like he was used to giving speeches before large crowds. He sounded like Grandpa Max, the former cop who had once made a name for himself. Howard's voice was similar but, perhaps, more expansive.

"I'm here, too, Alex," came Larry's voice. "We're on speaker." Larry Coates the obvious.

It was getting late and I was suddenly quite weary. That comes from having the floor pulled out from under one. Who knows when I would have another opportunity to swap war stories with the great Dominick Fennaday. So: "Larry. Sometime you'll have to tell me how you tracked my cousin down. But right now I need to ask Howard: Why did you come up to me in the subway and talk to me? What did you want?"

Howard laughed at his end. Annoying as hell. I thought back over his walking over to me in the subway just a few days ago: a little guy with a mustache, tiny half-lidded eyes, yapping at me. He was annoying then, too.

"Sorry, Alex," he said. "That was sort of a fluke. I spotted you on the street when you were walking on Broadway toward the subway. But it wasn't exactly by accident."

"What do you mean?"

"Well, I work uptown. Barney's Men's Suits on Broadway and West 76th. I had been going down to Levinson's Bookstore on 56th

Street lotsa times, hoping to catch you there. I saw you the other night when you were reading your novel."

"I don't get it," I said, still puzzling over his approaching me on the subway car at the beginning of last week. That was two days before my reading at Levinson's; two days before Tracy Lessing . . . "Why didn't you come over to me when I was signing books?"

"Well, frankly, I felt embarrassed – you know -- kidding you on the subway about your novel."

"Kidding me?"

"Yeah. Y'see, Alex, I've seen your books for years in store windows and places and always wondered if *that* Alex Brocton, the writer that people talked about, was my little cousin. I never read none of your books." A pause. "Sorry about that. I'm not much of a reader."

"So you got up the nerve to come over to me in the subway, pretending you read my novel, just for fun?"

"I wanted to be sure it was you. I only saw your picture on the back cover of your book and I thought maybe it was you. But how can anybody tell from a picture? I haven't seen you since you were a little kid, you know?"

"And you decided it was me?"

"Yeah. Sure I did. Not so much the voice. More like the *way* you talked. And that little gap between your front teeth. That clinched it. I was sure, then."

"What about the note?"

"What note?"

I heard Larry's voice muttering, "The one I showed you. From someone who said he was watching Alex and wanted to help. Signed 'Mr. Quiver.'"

"Oh, that," Howard said. "Yeah. No. That's not me. I didn't write it."

"What about Mr. Quiver?" I asked.

"Nope. Don't know it."

"But it was your father who made him up, didn't he?"

"Maybe he did. But I hadn't heard the story until Mr. Coates told me. Anyway, isn't Mr. Quiver supposed to be a protector or sumpthin? Mr. Coates here says that my dad made it up to be some kinda protector for your mom as a kid, isn't that it, Alex?"

"That's it," said Larry. "That's what your dad told you, right, Alex?"

"Yes," I replied. I was feeling disappointed and increasingly irritated listening to both Larry AND Howard. Could two such exasperating men be in the same room together and not explode to smithereens? "So, Howard, you don't know anything about a big man with black hair and eyes that are set far apart?"

"Nope. I don't know anybody like that. He Mr. Quiver? Or pretendin' to be?"

"I honestly don't know. Howard, I need to speak to Larry – Mr. Coates – for a moment in private. Do you mind?"

"Not at all."

"Yes, Alex," came Larry's voice. "This is Larry. Larry Coates."

See what I mean? Damned exasperating. "Larry, now we know that it's that big guy who helped me when I was being mugged. Jaime was his first name. James. Son of Mom's lover. Do you think you can find him?"

"I can try. But, so what? He hasn't done anything wrong. What do I do if I find him?"

"I just want to talk to him. Find out what he wants. Okay?"

"Sure, Alex. I'll call you next week. Even if I don't get anywhere. Wednesday okay?"

"Sure. Thanks for connecting me to my cousin. I appreciate that."

"It'll be on my bill," he answered with a chuckle. He clicked off.

I stuffed my phone into my jacket and then froze. I caught a glimpse of a man sitting on a sofa across from me, reading a magazine. It was the briefest of glimpses before he lifted the magazine in front of his face.

Large meaty head with tousled black hair, dark eyes far apart. His eyes on me.

CHAPTER SEVENTEEN
The World Went Away

Mr. Quiver's far apart dark eyes burned into me. I felt the heat searing me. He was there. Right there. I burned to lunge at him. *What do you want?*

I pressed my white-knuckled hands against the armrest of the cushioned chair and pushed myself up.

What do you want from me? Why are you following me?

My head throbbed as I rose.

"Daddy!" A little girl ran to the seated man holding the magazine. He lowered the magazine and got up. Yes, he had unkempt black hair and far apart eyes. But he was a short stubby man with a broad grin who embraced the little girl.

Red herring. I know – unfair to build up to a critical moment only to give you a false alarm. But that's real life. Sometimes.

Standing there like the fool I was, I took a half-dozen deep breaths and slowly eased the tension in my shoulders. The man and his daughter walked toward the elevators, never noticing the young fool standing across from them.

I looked around. People passed by while I stood shaking, unnoticed. I was inconsequential. Nothing at all. No one even glanced in my direction, wondering about me. With a self-conscious grin, I shook my head and tramped toward the elevators.

Sleep.

I was sound asleep, dreaming of Tracy Lessing, nude beside me. She smoothed my face, softly talking to me. "How does this feel?" she asked, cradling my head in the crook of her arm, pressing me into her bare breast. "How does this feel?"

Tracy jammed her rock-solid arm tightly around my skull. Pressure. Too tight. Couldn't get my breath. "Too much," I muttered. Tightening. "Too much. Too much. Hurting me."

"Hurting --" I sat up in a sweat. "-- me." I stared into the dimness, remembering. Hotel room. Science fiction convention. Dreaming.

My head hurt.

"What the hell," I said aloud. The screech of an alarm pierced the room. "What the hell is that?" I threw my covers aside and jumped out of bed. The phone was ringing and I thought if I could just get to it and pick it up the damn alarm would stop.

"Hello?" I yelled into the phone. My watch read two ten. The alarm blared on. "Who is this?"

"Desk. That's the fire alarm ringing. Fire Department will be here soon. Please leave your room and go to the lobby immediately."

"What the --" The line clicked off and the phone was dead in my hand. Shakily, I slipped on my eyeglasses. I pulled on pants and shirt, stepped into my shoes without socks, grabbed wallet and keys, took my tweed out of the closet, and left the room.

The alarm still sounding, I watched as sleepy-eyed groups of people hurried past, heading toward the lobby. A middle-aged man brushed hard against my shoulder, looked angrily at me, and grumbled, "Don't stand around. Lobby's this way." He moved on, racing down the long hallway.

I lumbered forward and picked up speed as I joined the traffic flow. The blare of the alarm and the flashing red light suffusing the hallway hurt my eyes. Trying to clear them, I saw the fear in others as they surged around me. I was left disoriented and confused – and feeling alone -- amid the rushing crowds.

"This way," shouted a young man who stepped out of a cross corridor. He grabbed my arm, stopping me with a jolt. "Help me. Please."

I could read extreme nervousness in the young man's face. Not fear, exactly. Something different. I fixed my glasses and realized that this man looked familiar.

"It's my mother," he cried. "She can't walk. Help me."

"Where is she?" I asked.

"This way." He half pulled my arm as he led me down the side corridor toward the rooms.

I pulled free of his grasp but continued walking close behind him. Tall and lanky, he had on khakis and a long-sleeved blue shirt, the shirt-tails hanging and the front unbuttoned. He was barefoot. I watched him warily as my eyesight adjusted to the flashing red lights. "Do I know you?"

"Me? I don't know. It's this door. Gotta find my key."

He was a couple of inches taller than me, blonde-haired, long wet strands hanging over his face. I caught sight of sharp blue eyes, a perfect chin, and grimly pressed lips.

"I know you," I shouted, just as the door clicked open and he pushed it in. "You're Dennis. We spoke at my reading at Levinson's. Dennis . . . something."

We stood at the threshold of the room and I gazed inside. I thought I saw something move near the open bathroom door. Light and shade were exchanged. But then, nothing. From my vantage, I clearly saw the bed. Nobody there. Dennis touched my elbow and we stepped into the room. The door clicked shut behind us. At a push from Dennis, I fairly tripped on the room's carpet.

"I prefer Dylan," he said. "Dylan --"

"Lance. I remember. Your mother in the ba --?"

I knew it. One second too late. I had sensed a black swirling tornado in his mind – a deliberately hidden hatred welling up out of Dennis. What I visualized was the image of an enveloping ink-black cloak spreading outward from him. I ducked, falling clumsily forward.

He gave me a solid blow just behind my ear. Pain exploded through my skull. I tumbled forward, reached the foot of a cushioned chair, and started to pull myself up. My glasses hung askew, hanging from one ear. My arms felt too numb to lift.

Heart pounding, fear choking me, I looked in his direction, my eyes moist and blurry.

Unable to focus, I shouted, "What do you want?"

"Now?" he screamed back. He was on one knee close to my right and swung at me. His fist jolted hard into my eye and forehead. My glasses dropped to the carpet as I fell backward.

"You're a smart man," he went on. "Now you're asking what I want? You couldn't care less when I pleaded with you to look at my manuscript. But now. Now! What do I want!"

Feeling helpless, I held up my arms as he pummeled me with his fists. One thing was consistently before my eyes. The rippled muscles of his stomach through his unbuttoned shirt. He was stronger than me. By far. Holding back his hands and wrists, I confronted hardened muscle. He'd floor me easily in this fight. And I couldn't keep him off me much longer.

He got up suddenly and stepped out of sight. I caught a few breaths on the floor. I didn't even try to find my eyeglasses. Sitting, I grabbed hold of a night table and pulled myself up. The drawer came open. Oh, good. The Bible. Suitable weapon. Do I throw it at him? Or read it aloud? Maybe he'll come to rapt attention if I do.

I sensed him coming fast behind me. Heart pumping, adrenaline racing through my body, I pushed myself up with my knee and swung around.

It wasn't a mighty roar, no Tarzan yell, but I did give a loud incoherent scream as I leapt at him. I cried out, "No more!" and swung the Gideon Bible into his face. It caught him at the point of his chin. I saw blood well from the gash.

He stepped back, surprised, and I shouted, "I'm getting out of here!"

I pushed him aside and made for the door. I reached the door handle, pulled at it.

Something hard slammed down onto the top of my head. My head felt soft and spongy. It seemed broken into splinters. But that was nothing –

His voice came from a million miles away: "You're not going anywhere!"

And then I hurt. Blood slid down my forehead and moist fingers of red touched my eyes. Time agonized backwards and I watched myself dying in three different instances – all in reverse. Four years ago: I saw myself tumble inside my parents' car in a fiery crash, Mom driving, on the way to the airport. Twelve years ago: the crazed gunman in Monticello who walked into my parents' shop slowly turning his pistol toward my sixteen-year old self and the blast rose up at me. Twenty-five years before: I struggled helplessly in Big Boy's bare arm as he held me by the neck above the concrete pool when I was three years old. My several deaths played back over and over as hotwire pain ripped through me, mind, body, and soul.

And then the world went away.

CHAPTER EIGHTEEN
Death Wouldn't Be so Bad If it Weren't for the Hours

So this was death. I can't say I liked it very much. At the time I couldn't say much of anything, for that matter. While I was there, I didn't have a thought. I mean, nothing. No sense of time passing, no flashes of my life, no profound insights of life or death, no visitors – spiritual or otherwise, and absolutely no sense of me.

It wasn't like being asleep. It was total nothingness. No end, no beginning, no sense of reaching a destination, no sense in *any* sense at all. There WAS no plane of existence elsewhere!

Think of it this way: in all the thousands of years of human history – since human history had been set down – there had been no 'you.' Not even a hint of you in existence anywhere. Unless you follow the beliefs of a well-known actress of the twentieth century who believed she had been reincarnated many times in the past and lived now merely in her latest incarnation – there simply was no YOU in existence in all of previous history. So why would you have the notion that you would come to exist as some kind of spirit or consciousness AFTER your body functions stop and you, once again, cease to exist in the world? We're blessed with this short span of time on earth and that's it. Why can't any of us find simple comfort in the fact that after we die we rejoin the molecules of the universe? I could find comfort in that.

I must admit I hadn't given any of this any thought while I was . . .away. Nothing like thought can exist if there is no ego. I didn't have any sense of fear – there was no 'I' and therefore no fear – but afterward, yes, sometime afterward, I was terrified that there would be no waking. I mean, no waking – forever.

I've been here before. And there it was. Out of blackness and blankness was the thought. Me. I. Waking.

"Alex!" Soft furry spoken syllables rising out of the depths. "He's . . . moving."

My eyes wouldn't open. But something gray passed my field of vision in the deep black. I wanted to grab that form. I wanted to grasp something outside of me me me. Pull myself back. Reel myself in.

"I . . . hurt." I heard my own voice, coming from a great distance. "Do . . . you . . .hear . . .me?"

Yes! Yes, I hear you! Dad? Is that . . .

I still couldn't open my eyes, like they were glued shut. I struggled to see, to know, to feel. *There! My eyelids fluttered. Yes, I did that! I'm awake. I'm aware. I feel . . .dull throbbing pain – meds in my system. Goodbye Death, old friend. Catch you some other time. Some long time from now.*

A hand touched my shoulder. Warm touch. Dad. "How do you feel, son?"

Like a dried out rag, I wanted to say. *Helpless as a tadpole in a raindrop.*

"You'll be all right. Rest now. We're here with you. Rest."

I slept the sleep of the almost dead. It was a good sleep, soft and pleasant.

"See? His eyelids are moving! Hey, Alex! It's me."

Not ready for this. Let me sleep a bit more.

"C'mon, Alex! I know you're awake. It's Larry. Larry Coates."

I know. That's Coates with a silent 'e.'

No use. I opened my eyes. Yep, there he was. Larry Coates. Standing with a big grin on his face. Aly was right there beside him, looking nervous, moist channels lining her face. From my bed – hospital bed? – I didn't see Dad.

"Hello." I whispered. I tried for more but couldn't get any farther.

"Top of your head looks damn ugly, Alex," Larry said.

Aly slapped his shoulder and turned to me. "The doctors say you don't have a fracture. They say you're healing well."

"Yeah," Larry chimed in, "They say you got the hardest damn-ass head they'd ever seen. They're gonna toss you out of here any time now."

Aly gave a worn smile and scratched her chin. "You're in a hospital in Philadelphia. But the doctors here aren't ready to discharge you yet. They're conferring with Dad right now. We'll see."

My eyes grew cloudy so that I saw Aly and Larry through increasing cobwebs. I tried to speak: "Tired." *But tell me, what happened?* So many questions.

"We'll let you rest, Alex," said Aly. "We'll be back in the morning. When we tell Dad you're awake, he'll be busting a gut wanting to see you."

Larry patted my shoulder. "See you tomorrow, old man."

As my heavy eyelids covered my vision, I saw Aly press her head against Larry's chest and Larry slip his arm around her.

Aly's married to Brian last I heard. What the hell you doing, Larry?

CHAPTER NINETEEN
The Mind-Body Connection

Someone was in my room! Sitting beside my bed. Someone I didn't know, keeping an eye on me while looking over papers. I sensed that it was a male in a suit and he was reading a report – a report about me!

All this without opening my eyes. I've always had a very advanced body-mind connection. I know that people are present and taking action around me even when I'm barely conscious. This person beside me had just leaned toward me and slapped my wrist hard. He intended that I wake up. I felt his impatience. And his curiosity.

"How are you feeling today, Mr. Brocton?"

The man who spoke sat in a metallic upright chair next to my hospital bed. He was holding some papers on a clipboard in front of him. He uncrossed his legs and straightened, then took off half-framed reading glasses. His face was well-tanned and had a ready smile. He had curled black hair that was so dark and wiry that I've heard it called jet black. As he stuck his folded glasses into the breast pocket of his gray suit, he stared at me with fierce blue eyes.

He reached out with a massive hand and touched my arm. "Feel able to talk, Mr. Brocton?"

My mouth felt dry but – "I think so." I surprised myself. I sounded almost normal. "Where – what hospital . . ?"

"You're in Hahnemann University Hospital. Philadelphia."

"Still Philly. What time is it?"

"Late. The nurse just left after taking some blood. You slept right through it."

That was a lie. No one had come in to draw blood. My wrist still stung from the slap he gave me. It put me on my guard.

"Where's my father? Sister?"

"They left hours ago. You needed your sleep. Do you feel up to talking to me?"

"Sure. Doctor --?"

"My name is Ambrose. Stanley Ambrose. My colleague here" – he pointed to a young woman wearing a white smock who was seated in a chair at the foot of my bed; she was shapely and had short blonde hair and wore silver-framed glasses – "This is Colleen Daugherty. She's going to take some notes as we talk. That okay?"

"Yeah. Okay. But tell me: how am I doing?"

"Remarkably well, I hear. Considering the beating you took. Do you remember anything about that?"

I wasn't reading Ambrose. And I got nothing from his colleague either. That has happened in the past. Often I can't see what's in people's minds until they become familiar to me. Mind reading isn't an exact science. And strangers remain unknown to me – until I listen for a while. Still, I knew that this man was holding things back.

"My glasses," I said. "Anybody find them in the hotel room?"

Ambrose reached around to the mobile table against the wall. "Here they are. Your sister identified them as yours."

He handed them to me and I slipped them on. I sat back and used the button to raise the upper part of the bed.

My glasses. They're not helping me read anything in him. Nothing in Ambrose nor the young woman. Is it possible that this beating caused me to lose my special ability? Still, I do sense things from him. Feelings. He's irritated with my slowness. He wants something definite from me. I sense that, as if I can smell it on him. The sensation's tangible -- smells something like vinegar – sour and slick.

"So," Ambrose said, "you remember you were in a hotel room. What happened there?"

"Guy beat the shit out of me."

"Why? What led to that?"

"Okay. Let me think. There was a fire alarm in the middle of the night. How long ago was that, Doctor?"

"That was Friday the twelfth. Today's Tuesday. So, four days ago. Did you know the guy?"

"Yes. A fan. He called himself Dylan Lance. But his real name, he told me, was Dennis Leibowitz. He came to my last book reading at Levinson's in New York. He got angry at me when I refused to read a manuscript he brought with him. I suppose that was his reason for attacking me at the convention."

"Why'd you go with him?"

"What?" I hadn't expected that. This Ambrose was definitely after something. And he was keeping something from me. "Dylan, or Dennis, stopped me in the hallway during the fire alarm, claiming he needed help with his mother. I recognized him from the signing, so I went with him. Wouldn't you have done the same?"

Ambrose rubbed his eyes, looked at the woman taking notes, and back to me. "Maybe. And maybe not. So you weren't suspicious? You had no idea that it was a trick of some kind?"

"No. I don't usually think that way."

"What way?"

"That people are out to get me. Do you, Doctor?"

Ambrose winced as if I had physically hurt him. I watched in surprise mainly because I felt as if I *did* hurt him.

"Let's get back to you, Mr. Brocton. Do you know what Mr. Leibowitz hit you with?"

"His fists mostly. He's stronger than me. By far. I hit him with a Bible. I think it must've smarted." I chuckled inwardly but Ambrose didn't seem to get the joke. "But Dennis must've told the police all this already. Unless Dennis is on the run and hasn't been caught. Do you know if he's under arrest?"

Ambrose appeared to struggle with the question and I knew then he was holding back something vital. Finally, he asked, "Do you know what he hit you with – ultimately?"

"Something damn heavy. But I didn't see what. What was it?"

"Some sort of trophy. Heavy rectangular pedestal, rounded backing with embossed stars, some kind of flying saucer raised out from the background."

My Infinity Award! I won that two years ago at NestaCon in Boston.

Ambrose stared closely at my face. "Based on the medical reports --" He held up the clipboard in his hand – "he must've held it around the top and struck you with the base. Otherwise the jagged edges would've smashed your skull into jelly."

"Not something I want to think about," I murmured.

"Do you know what it was, Mr. Brocton?"

"Yes," I answered. "An award I received some time ago."

"How did he get his hands on it?"

"I don't know. It was in my apartment before I left for the convention. At least, I thought so. Do you know anything about it, *Doctor* Ambrose?"

Ambrose dropped the clipboard and bent to retrieve it. When he sat up, his face was shiny from perspiration.

I asked, "You all right?"

"Yes," he said. He took a breath and his gaze on me hardened. "If you knew that trophy was missing, Mr. Brocton, you would probably have expected to see someone like Dennis Leibowitz at the convention. Someone who was out to get you? Wouldn't you?"

"I don't see why. And I didn't realize my award was missing. But I'm beginning to think you're keeping something secret. Something I should know. Are you even a doctor?"

He winced again as if trying to fight an oncoming headache. It seemed like cause-and-effect, like I was causing that headache.

His associate, Colleen what's-her-name, stopped taking notes and stared wide-eyed at him. "Ambrose?" she said.

He pointed a finger at her. "It's okay." He turned back to me. "Someone else was there, isn't that true? Someone who helped you fight off Leibowitz. Who was it?"

"No, there wasn't anyone else. Dennis beat me to a pulp and I was knocked out. I woke up here. That's it. Unless you know anything more. Who are you? Really?"

"I'm Detective Stanley Ambrose of the 22nd District here in Philly." He blinked twice as if he couldn't believe he was saying the words.

"What's with all these questions?" I asked.

"Ambrose!" his female colleague called sharply.

He waved his hand toward her. "We've been assigned to investigate the murder."

That shook me. "Who was murdered?"

"Dennis Leibowitz."

CHAPTER TWENTY
We Don't Possess All of the Facts

I stared at Detective Stanley Ambrose of the Philadelphia Police Department from my hospital bed, feeling as if I'd dreamt up our entire conversation. But it hadn't been a dream. His sharp blue eyes were fixed on me. Real, definitely real. My throat tightened and I couldn't swallow.

Dennis Leibowitz is dead? And this man thinks I'm guilty somehow?

This cop couldn't be for real! Dennis was bigger and stronger than me. He had smashed in my brains. I was unconscious. But – well, maybe -- there could have been someone else there. I remembered I saw something like movement in the bathroom.

Mister Quiver.

"Well, Mr. Brocton?" Ambrose said, his eyes burning into mine. "Were you alone when you went to Leibowitz's room? Or not?"

"Dennis took me by surprise," I answered. "I didn't have anyone with me. Why? Do you think that someone else could have been hiding in his room?"

Ambrose glared at me. "You saying there was?"

Is he kidding me? "I don't know. Dennis went after me, remember? I didn't have any way to take him on." *How could I have taken the guy? He was more muscular than me. I couldn't overpower him.*

"You could have used a knife," Ambrose said.

What, was Ambrose reading MY mind now? Where'd he pull that comment from?

"I didn't have a knife. I never carry a knife."

"You could have used the knife he was carrying," he continued. "His own knife."

"Detective!" said his colleague. She stood and tossed her notes and eyeglasses onto the chair. Her green eyes flared as she spoke. "Don't say anything. We're still working the case."

"I know that!" Ambrose retorted, standing to face her.

My pulse raced in my neck. These two scared the hell out of me. What's going on between them?

"Maybe you two should take it outside," I said.

Ambrose stared at me, his voice bitingly sharp, "I want the truth out of you!"

"Stanley!" Daugherty called out. "Step back. Mr. Brocton hasn't done anything wrong."

"He's holding something back," he retorted.

"Take a breath, Detective. Now!" The woman looked at me. "It's all right," she said. Her voice was even. "We don't always see eye to eye." She gave me a thin-lipped smile that I knew was forced.

She meant for me to stay calm. It wasn't working. My eyes felt tired and I took off my glasses to rub them. Looking at my two visitors, I realized my vision was quite clear and sharp. I held my glasses folded in my hand.

I had a good look at Colleen Daugherty then. She was older than I thought at first glance. Her deeply-lined eyes held Ambrose in a penetrating stare; creases delineated a mature, thoughtful face; her blonde hair was splotched with gray and was pulled back severely from her forehead. Something in this woman's bearing expressed an uncommon strength. I read in their relative positions, in the look on their faces, in their attitudes, that she had more authority than Ambrose. I sensed that she deliberately let him do the talking while she listened and gathered information from me.

I got it wrong. Ambrose isn't in charge here. She is.

"What happened in that room, Mr. Brocton?" asked Colleen Daugherty.

"Dennis Leibowitz beat the shit out of me. Then hit me over the head with something. Your partner here just told me it was an award I received. Mr. Ambrose said Dennis stole that from my apartment. Clearly, you know more about it than I do."

Ambrose burst out with: "Clearly!" His face instantly showed regret as Daugherty glared at him.

My face felt hot. I wanted them out of here but I also wanted to know what happened. My stomach was churning like a washing machine.

"Tell me what happened to Dennis," I said. *Tell me and get out!*

"We found him lying face up on the bed. He was stabbed twice," Ambrose spewed out. "Once in the stomach and once in the upper chest."

"Shut up, Detective!" Daugherty said sharply.

"No, I really want to know," I said. "I have a right to know."

"Yeah," spoke up Ambrose. "He has a right to know."

I gazed at him. Was he being sarcastic? Or had I somehow persuaded him?

Daugherty's eyes softened as she looked at me. "We don't possess all of the facts, Mr. Brocton." Good cop, bad cop. Like on TV. But was she trying to be the good cop? Was Ambrose the cop that turned on a dime? Bad cop? I didn't know. I was too damn scared to know exactly what the hell was going on.

"What facts," I began, "do you know?"

"We found something," said Ambrose.

Daugherty called, "No. We don't know."

"What is it?" I asked. I looked from one to the other. "Please."

Ambrose: "Something Leibowitz was holding."

Daugherty: "It's nothing."

"What was it?"

"Something . . ."

"No. We don't know."

"Please tell me."

"What are you doing here?" came from a nurse who suddenly appeared. "Who are you?"

I saw who she was without the need to put on my glasses. "Nurse," I said, using my elbows to sit up. "One moment." I looked at the detectives and gathered my strength. "What was Dennis holding?"

Daugherty glowered – at me, at Ambrose, at the nurse.

"A torn bit of a shirt, bloody," said Ambrose. "From a shirtsleeve. With a button."

"Can you figure out anything from it?" I asked.

"Nothing," said Daugherty. "It's Leibowitz's blood."

I saw it in Ambrose's mind. The torn bit of sleeve didn't have an ordinary shirt button. It wasn't round, for one thing. It was green in color. And shaped like a four-leaf clover.

It's from a woman's blouse!

CHAPTER TWENTY-ONE
Tell Me Everything

Exhilarating! Yes! Thrilling! Yes! Scary as hell! Yes!

I breathed rapidly in excitement as I watched Ambrose and Daugherty leaving. I felt the nurse's eyes on me as my face heated up and my chest sped in and out. My hands shook with shuddering delight. I couldn't cool down, couldn't stop my rushing breath, couldn't stop my shaking.

"Are you all right?" asked the nurse. Her name was Renee. She had been taking care of me the previous evening and we had gotten along well. Besides, she was twenty-four and single – though she had a boyfriend; they all do – and was quite pleasant in every way. But my mind was racing over what had just happened.

I was in control! I mean, I was in control of that detective. Ambrose. His real name, undoubtedly. Although he hadn't shown me any identification. He was ready to tell me everything! I had gotten into his head! He couldn't lie to me. I've become some kind of human lie detector.

Yes! I was a superhero and I had a new superpower. Thanks to that smash to my head. Thanks to being killed by a crazed fan and then returned to life. What was it I now had? Oh, yes, of course. Super Duper truth-telling power. Wonder Woman had her lasso to force the truth out of criminals. But I could do it without a device of any kind. What to call it? Candor extraction? Okay, not catchy. But you couldn't keep any secrets from me! I'm Super Candor Extractor!!

The detective told me about evidence they found. The bloody shirtsleeve with a button. I got Ambrose to show it to me in his mind. I'm sure I drew it out of him. The man simply wouldn't have kept images of shirtsleeves in his head. And I knew it was the truth. He couldn't NOT reveal it to me.

But Daugherty was something else. I couldn't reach her.

A woman's bloody sleeve with a button shaped like a four-leaf clover . . .

That happened sometimes. There were people I couldn't read. Women more than men, now that I thought about it.

A woman was there, in Dennis's room . . .

But I hadn't made a study of it. Maybe I should keep track. Score the number of women to men whose minds I could read. It could be very useful data.

Mr. Quiver hadn't been working alone. A woman was with him. Who was she . .?

Start a statistical study to be applied to clusters of people under controlled conditions. Sure. Join a medical institution performing clinical research. Maybe I should publish.

Yeah, and find myself locked in a cage running through mazes while pimple-faced undergraduate students study ME!

I slipped on my eyeglasses and looked up at the nurse. Oddly, the view of the room grew vague, her features less sharp.

Nurse Renee leaned over me and touched my forehead. Her white blouse was down by three buttons. I shifted in the bed to see a tad more of the breasts bulging against that blouse. My glasses became fogged and I took them off. I saw a lot more clearly without them.

"Your head is very warm," Renee said. "I'll take your temperature. And your blood pressure."

"Thanks, Renee." Why should I argue with a trained nurse?

After Renee took my temperature and my blood pressure, she took the added precaution of holding my wrist to check my pulse. And then she reached under my flimsy hospital gown to press her hand (cool hand) against my chest. "Heart's good," she said with a smile.

I smiled back. Her heart was good too. At least her chest was. Breathed in and out real good. Nearly popped open the fourth button on her blouse.

Buttons. A button shaped like a four-leaf clover on a torn and bloodied sleeve clasped in Dennis Leibowitz's dead hand. Who was the woman? Was she there with my Mr. Quiver? Or was she there with Dennis but turned on him? She had to have helped in Dennis's death if he had been in close contact sufficiently to rip off that sleeve. Why was she there? For me? Why?

The button popped open on Nurse Renee's blouse and she laughed.

Straightening, Renee murmured, "I think you've seen enough, Alex."

"Are you teasing me?"

"Maybe," she answered, and proceeded to button all of them. "Just a little."

Did she say that to be coy? Or was I influencing her to respond truthfully? Dear sweet nurse Renee, what's on your mind?

She turned away, pressing her fingers to her forehead, as if she had a sudden headache. *Did I do that?*

"You okay?" I asked.

"Yes. It was a twinge, all of a sudden. Gone now." She turned away to head to the door. "Have to make my rounds. Other patients need attention, too."

But I had to see the extent of my -- "What's your boyfriend's name?"

"Craig," she answered, looking back at me, as if she was forced to say his name before she could do what she intended, which was to leave.

"What does he do for a living?"

"He's an intern at Thomas Jefferson Hospital. He's planning to be a surgeon."

"Do you like him?"

"Do I --" She stared at me, her eyes showing equal parts anger and confusion. "He's not serious about anything. Makes jokes all the time. Doesn't know what field he wants to specialize in. Wants me to call him Hawkeye like the character in M*A*S*H. Not serious about me. No, I'm not happy about any of that."

Intriguing. She was saying more than she needed to in response to my question. That must be because of me. I'm drawing her out. Making it a compulsion.

"I'd take you seriously, Renee." A little earnest dishonesty goes a long way. As long as she couldn't read *my* mind. "We should get together after I'm out of here."

"You live in New York. I'm in Philly."

"It's not so far. I come here for signings all the time."

"I don't date patients."

"But I'd like to hear what you think of my books. You know I'm a novelist, don't you? Haven't you heard of me? Seen my novels?"

"Yes, Alex. I know who you are. I don't spend much time reading science fiction but I've read your last novel, <u>Evolved Parameters.</u>"

"Really?" I was a bit surprised. It seemed too good to be true. "What did you think of it?"

"It had its moments."

"Tell me the truth. Did you really like it?"

Renee's eyebrows lowered in reflection. "I found it a disappointing read."

"What?"

"The concluding chapters don't carry the earlier parts' excitement."

"But the whole novel is about an evil force causing people to change. That went on throughout the entire novel. Didn't you think that was exciting?"

"The changes that come over the main characters aren't particularly interesting. The ending left me hanging."

"But I purposely left the final scene open-ended. You were meant to want more."

"But even before that, the plot was getting a little dull."

I was flabbergasted. *Was she putting me on? Or was she being compelled to tell me the pure truth? How could she NOT like my novel?*

"So . . ." I tried to find a way to assess whether or not she believed what she was saying. "You didn't find Kingston's transformation as his part of the story progressed exciting? You didn't find the change in him shocking?"

"Kingston does have some appeal for me but he loses that when he slowly transforms into a perfect gentleman who blithely helps people he meets. I lost interest rather quickly after that." She looked at her watch. "Oh, I've got to check on Mrs. Perelson. She needs help with her medicine. I'll look in on you later, Alex."

I was breathing rapidly again, my face aflame and pulsing. I tried on my glasses again and tossed them off in disgust. Oh, yes, I had a superpower all right. I was able to draw out the truth from people. Great! And it didn't matter whether I wanted to hear the truth or not. I got it right in the face.

I was left scared out of my mind.

CHAPTER TWENTY-TWO
Next Steps

After finishing my breakfast of tasteless scrambled eggs, bland home fries, cold wheat toast with hard butter, thin coffee, and sour orange juice, I shuttled my intravenous pole and myself into the tiny bathroom to urinate. Suddenly I remembered I had left my eyeglasses on the mobile table with the remains of breakfast.

No need to get them now. I washed my hands and looked at my face in the mirror. *Nurse Renee didn't like my novel. Did she like me? At all?* Hair wildly unkempt, several days' stubble on my cheeks, eyes bloodshot. A swath of taped padding firmly pressed against the top of my head. "You look like you'd be a charming date for any girl," I said out loud, feeling sorry for myself. The face looking back didn't have an answer.

Instead of getting back into bed, I got my smart phone out of my crushed plastic hospital bag containing my personal belongings, sat on one of the two chairs near the bed, and looked at my contacts. I tapped a familiar number.

"Hey, old man," answered Larry Coates. "Saw your ID on my phone. How you doing, Alex?"

"I'm okay. Are you still in Philadelphia?"

"No. I'm in my New York office. Got a full day ahead."

"Well, Larry, I've got to tell you: two Philly cops visited me here in the hospital."

"Cops? When?"

"About half hour ago. Detectives. Did you fuckin' know that the guy who attacked me is dead?"

"Well, yeah, I did. Aly told me. I think she got it out of a uniformed cop at the hospital. You weren't really up to hearing about it when I saw you yesterday so I kept quiet."

Yeah. I remember yesterday. Alyson snuggling up to you. A little too close . . .

Larry continued, "Let me write this down: What were the names of the detectives?"

"Ambrose and Daugherty. Daugherty's a woman. I can't think of her first name. But . . . Stanley. Stanley Ambrose."

"Spell the names." I did. Then Larry went on, "Do you know where they work out of?"

"They didn't bother to tell me."

"No worries. I'll track them down."

When did Aly and you start getting so close, Larry? I ached to ask. Instead, I asked a different burning question: "So you knew the guy – Dennis Leibowitz – was killed? Do you know anything more about it?"

"No. There's nothing in the media about it. I sometimes use a detective still with the NYPD. Haven't called him yet. Guess I'll do that first chance I get. Anything else this Detective Ambrose tell you?"

"Yeah. He thinks I had help, someone who was with me."

"So, this Ambrose simply said that, said it out loud to you."

"No, he didn't." *What the hell's on your mind, Larry?* "What are you thinking?"

"So the detectives don't know about your . . . mental thing?"

"Hell no!" *That summer in Monticello, Aly hung around us. Was it because she had a thing for you?* "You haven't spoken about it, have you?"

"No. You know I wouldn't."

"Okay, Larry." *Can I read you through the phone? No, of course not. You're two hundred miles away and this is a mechanical device I'm holding.*

"So . . ." here Larry paused as if in deep thought. I suspected that he was unable to think of a thing. Just hot air between his ears. "I think you'd better tell the police."

"Here in Philly?" That scared the shit out of me. "Tell them what?"

"About the note you got from Mr. Quiver."

Shit shit shit! "If I tell these detectives about Mr. Quiver, I'll have to tell them about my ability to read people. How else could I explain his interest in helping me?"

"Look, this is no longer a situation of idle curiosity on our part. This is a murder investigation. I don't see how you can avoid telling them about the note signed Mr. Quiver saying that . . ." Here I heard some shuffling of papers, ". . .that he knows you're special and 'will be around to help when you need it.' If you don't inform them, you could be charged with withholding evidence."

Uncontrollably, I shouted, "They'll never leave me alone!" I heard Larry's deep breathing on the other end of the line. It took a moment, but I composed myself. "You've got to find Jaime! He's the only one we know who could be Mr. Quiver. Or, at least, the one who's interceding on my behalf." *The woman's shirtsleeve! There is that! The bloody shirtsleeve! A woman was helping him.* "Why the hell haven't you been able to locate him?"

"Without his full name it's practically impossible for me to track him down. All the more reason to turn over the note and tell what you know to the cops."

"I need a little time to think it over, Larry. I think these detectives are going to check up on me. Maybe contact the New York police. You see, I . . ." *Hell! I don't want Larry to know that something's been added to my special ability. No telling . . .* "I can't explain to these detectives that someone has been watching me for years, someone who cared enough to save me when I was in danger in that hotel."

"But Alex, we can't avoid telling them what we know. If these two detectives pursue this and notify the NYPD – and the New York cops come knocking on my door, I'll have to -- And that note from Mr. Quiver is pertinent to the case. Besides, I don't see how else I can proceed. Unless *you* can locate this Jaime yourself . . ."

Find Mr. Quiver. That's the imperative. He may be watching me even while I'm here in the hospital. I know now that there's someone else, a woman. It's even possible that there are others. How do I find them? What can I do to get to them? How?

"I just had a crazy idea," said Larry. "It'll have to wait until after you get out of the hospital and back to New York. But then we would be able to put things in motion."

"What have you got in mind?"

"Let's put you in danger." Larry's voice cracked as he broke into a laugh.

My stomach twisted inside me. I couldn't read him over my phone but I could divine what was going on in that little brain of his, knowing Larry Coates.

"How dangerous?" I asked.

"Very. Well, not very. It has to be something in which someone watching would see it coming. Do you trust me?"

No! "Yes. What kind of danger do you have in mind?"

"I don't know. Haven't figured it out yet. It'll be something that we could devise and control. A danger that Mr. Quiver or whatever would be urged to rescue you from."

Damn! It was a clever way to move forward without informing the police. It would also prove that whoever it was WAS indeed watching me and wanted to keep me safe. If we were right about all of that. Just one thing –

I didn't like being a target. Not one bit.

CHAPTER TWENTY-THREE
The Plan

"**W**e've set up a bed for you in here," said Brian Gainer, leading the way. "Over there by the window is a cabinet we cleared out for your things."

The hospital administration wouldn't discharge me unless I agreed to being placed in someone's care in New York. And I had to be cleared by my family doctor at the end of ten days. I was remanded to the custody of my sister, who drove Dad and me from Philadelphia to her studio apartment in Lower Manhattan. Her husband Brian, who had returned to New York after his bridge tournament in Jersey, met me at the door. Aly and Dad went hunting for a parking space.

"I have to prepare some problems for my class tomorrow," Brian said. "Why don't you start unpacking and get acclimated."

"Sure. Thanks."

I'd never been friendly with Aly's husband. I couldn't read much of anything in Brian's mind. Numerals. That was what I saw. Living numerals twirling about in his brain. Dizzying, and I didn't like the vision. Just then, before he disappeared into the bedroom, several animated fours were in a mad dance around bulbous threes. Mad, indeed.

We were finishing Vietnamese take-out when Larry Coates called.

"Ask the warden," he said, "if you're free to come to my place in Chelsea for a little tete-a-tete." He had a small apartment he used for private business meetings a handful of blocks to the north. I relayed Larry's message.

Aly grabbed my cell phone. "On condition that I drive him there, Larry."

"Hi, Aly. No need. I'll come by and pick up the old man and bring him back, too. So, can Alex come out and play?"

'Twas agreed.

It was heavy dusk when Larry came around. He called from his car and I came out wearing my coat and leather gloves. I was also sporting my head bandage and walking with a metal cane that a doctor at the hospital had suggested and my sister had insisted upon. I found that my stride was shaky but I blamed that on my not being used to walking with a cane. I still didn't see the necessity of it.

When I opened the car door and pushed in beside him, fighting to place the cane between my legs, Larry eyed me. "That's a good look for you, old man," he said. "Where are your glasses?"

"Don't need them." I glared at Larry as I strapped in. I hated him. I hated his jesting and his abstracted manner and his ear-to-ear smile. I wanted to lash out at him.

"My sister," I began with quiet deliberate intensity. "Did you spend a lot of time with my sister at the hospital?"

"With Aly? We sat in the cafeteria and drank coffee and talked. Why?"

Why? Why? "The two of you seemed awfully friendly when you visited me. Aly does have a husband. She's married. What were you thinking?"

"Oh. I see. About that, I think you've got us wrong. That summer in Monticello when we were kids, Aly and I shared a chocolate thick shake once. I was feeling low. I didn't talk to you about it but my parents were getting a divorce. I felt alone and self-pitying. Aly let me open up to her. And that's all there was to it."

I stared at him. *What an ass I am!* Finally I said, "I wish I had known that. You were always kidding around – I didn't have an inkling. Sorry."

"That's all right. I like your sister. I'd still like to get into her pants!"

I punched him in the shoulder.

He turned on the ignition key, smiled, and said, "I've got the plan. Fully formed."

He pulled away and drove the avenues of Lower Manhattan like a maniac.

I cried out, "What are you doing?"

"Look in the side-view," he muttered.

He turned his wheel sharply and his tires squealed as he headed east, speeding through a street of Mom-and-Pop stores.

"What are you doing?"

"See anything behind us?" he asked.

I gasped out, "Like someone following us?" My chest heaved in fear.

"Like anything."

His speedometer raced to fifty-five on a one-way street lined with brownstones. Larry blew his horn at people crossing in front of us.

"What the hell are you doing, Larry?"

"Anything going on?"

"Yeah. People on the sidewalk are screaming at you."

"Any cars close behind?"

"No! Slow down or we'll have the cops coming after us with sirens blasting."

THAT stopped him. At least he slowed down to a city crawl. I gazed out the window and breathed deeply. We were heading toward the East River.

"Hey!" I burst out. "Why are we heading to the river?"

"We're not going to my apartment."

"Why not?"

"Because I don't want anybody to know where we *are* going." He pulled into a space at East River Park and got out.

I trudged out my side and asked, "What are we doing here?"

He gazed at me with his quirky dopey grin. "Wait. Let's walk."

He pulled up his fur collar and stuck his hands in his coat pockets, leading me onto the walkway, the choppy river to our left. Still not used to my cane, I managed to keep beside him as he increased to a rapid pace. He was silent as joggers ran past and infrequent couples strolled by, huddling close against the night breeze.

"So," he began, "how come you don't have to wear your glasses?"

"I can see without them. Getting my head bashed in must've changed my vision."

Considering that, Larry nodded. "We can't do anything criminal," he murmured, so low I scarcely heard. "So, the first thing is: we can't have someone using a weapon. No knives, no bats, no guns. Not even fake ones."

"And no cars. No hit-and-run."

"No cars. No motorcycles, trucks, bicycles or scooters. No vehicles of any kind. We can't have anyone accuse us of criminal wrong-doing."

"Okay. So, what's the plan you've cooked up?"

"It's got to seem accidental. An argument between people that builds into something more. That's all you need to know."

"How am I supposed to know when it happens?"

"Don't plan anything. It'll be something that's escalating as you come upon it. What happens will take a few minutes to give our guy time to consider stepping in."

Our guy. I liked the phrase. "How do I become involved?"

"You don't. Go with the flow when you see it coming your way. Got that? Don't back down. Don't resist. Stand your ground when things fall to you. Okay?"

"Sure. Now, look, I won't really be hurt, will I?"

"It's got to look real. Make sure you have your cane with you. Stumble around while you walk before anything happens. Look more fragile than you really are."

"Sure. I got you. Look, when our guy – Jaime or whoever – makes his move to rescue me, how are we going to overtake and hold him?"

"I'm arranging for more than one team to keep sight of you. I've got things worked out with the detective I sometimes use on legal cases. There'll be no official notification to the police. But that doesn't mean there won't be any cops around."

"Okay. When do we do this?"

"Whenever you go outside from here on. Where you would likely be watched."

"How the hell are you going to know that? If you follow me, our guy might spot that. Then, no one will step in to save me from anything."

"Here." He took out a small pin with an American flag insignia. A jogger was running toward us. Larry pushed the pin into my gloved hand. "Put it in your pocket."

I stuffed it into my coat as the jogger raced past.

I envisioned a camera just then, the image clearly directed at me. Looking at Larry, I caught his smile.

"Got it?" Larry asked.

"Yeah. It's a camera."

"What about the rest?" he asked, noticing my blank expression. "Did you hear what I was saying – my thought?"

"No. I don't hear words when I read people. Sometimes, I'll pick up the sounds that a person imagines in his thoughts. Nothing articulated as a message."

"Damn! Okay, look, every time you go out, wear the pin on your coat. Newest technology. Self-contained power source. Press the tab down and it will record whatever you see. And, unlike your telepathic thing, it will pick up sounds, words, what people are saying. It has a pretty good range, actually. Press the tab again so that it slides up and the camera shuts off. Got that?"

"Yes. Oh, what's the name of your detective friend?"

"Nope. You don't need to know. And I'm not showing you a picture of him, either. Don't bother reading my mind. It's closed to you. That's all, folks!"

"Okay, Larry. Will you be there when it happens?"

"Maybe. Maybe not. Probably not, Alex. Anyway, I'll be damn sure you don't see me there, even after we get him. Let's start back for the car."

As we headed back, he asked, "Any questions?"

"I think you covered everything. Oh! Maybe . . . just one."

"Go ahead."

"Do you think it'll work?"

"Sure. How else can we proceed?" He picked up the pace and I hurried along, clicking my cane against the pavement. He laughed, a good hearty unrestrained laugh.

"What?" I asked.

"It occurred to me just now. This little mission of ours? Our putting you in jeopardy? And working out your rescue by manipulating our guy?"

"What about it?"

"Well, on this assignment, I think that makes *me* 'Mr. Quiver.'"

CHAPTER TWENTY-FOUR
A Walk Through the Village

"I guess it's time for me to say goodbye, son."

My eyes grew moist as I said, "Can't you stay a few more days, Dad? I'm sure Aly will put you up a while longer."

Dad stood by the apartment door, long winter coat and hat on, carrying one large suitcase. "I've got to take care of some business home in Miami."

It lasted about fifteen seconds. The image of a woman with gray hair tied in a pony-tail. She was smiling, attractive in a mature way, slender in a long dress the color of turquoise, with earrings to match.

Dad's solemn eyes became dreamy while I saw this image. *Knew it. Dad's seeing someone in Florida. Living together? In sin? No, not Dad. Well . . .*

Abruptly, Dad's eyes steadied as he looked at me. He continued as if there was no pause, "Get back to my condo. Pay some bills. They won't take care of themselves." He smiled briefly. "Besides, I was only here because you needed me."

"I still need you."

"That's not true, Alex. You're healing quite well. You'll be getting back to your apartment in Queens in a couple of days, getting back to your usual routine. You'll forget I was ever here."

Perhaps he was right. No, not about forgetting his visit, not true at all. But I was itchy to get back to my own place. And get back to working in earnest. My new novel-in-progress had been neglected because I'd been anxious about 'the Mr. Quiver Mission,' as Larry liked calling it. Over the past three days, Larry called me numbers of times, usually after I had gone out and returned. Yes, I'd been out, taking walks, sitting in the park, once or twice alone but oftentimes with Dad. I had turned on the flag insignia pin on my coat lapel every time. Nothing happened – except for Larry's phone calls.

I looked at Dad standing there in quiet reserve, holding his suitcase steadfastly, and I felt the ache of knowing I would miss him terribly once he left.

"Perhaps," Dad was saying, "you'll come down to Florida for a visit this winter."

"I'd like that," I replied. "As soon as I finish this latest."

"Don't put it off too long, Alex. I'd --" The cell phone in Dad's coat sounded repeatedly. He pulled it out and answered: "Hello. Yes. Okay. I'll be right down. Yes, I'm ready. I have everything. See you in a minute. 'Bye."

Clearing my throat, I asked, "Aly?"

He nodded. "She's downstairs waiting in the car."

"How are you going?"

"Flying out of New Jersey. Aly's taking me to Newark. It's easier for her that way." He gave me a final assessment. "It's good you don't have to wear your glasses anymore. You're a handsome boy."

Dad put down the suitcase then and did something he hadn't done in years. He wrapped his arms around me and kissed my cheek. When he finished, he picked up his suitcase and gave me a smile. He covered the moisture on his face by turning away and walking to the door of the apartment.

"Good-bye, son," he managed, then he opened the door and left.

I felt at a loss as I scanned the apartment. *What should I do?* I walked toward my unmade cot and stared out the large window. I saw, far below, a car that might have been Aly's driving out the main gate. I drew in a long breath, feeling a bit sorry for myself. I was alone.

Well, not quite. Aly's husband, Brian, was in the bedroom. I presumed. I hadn't heard anything coming from there since we ate breakfast together earlier. As we ate, he mostly nodded at Aly and Dad as they discussed television, movies, sports, and everything else. He did say one thing to me when I talked about the alien presence in the novel I was writing. He said, "That sounds keen." These days, who says 'keen?' And what did he mean by that? Was he being sarcastic? Aly assured me afterward that he spoke literally and that Bri was 'most impressed' with me.

Although he and Aly had been married for – how long? – six years now? Yes, that's right. It was six years -- I was hardly close with Brian. He was an odd one. An adjunct professor at Manhattan Community College who, Aly said, was a math whiz, but left no impression on me of genius whatsoever. He wasn't much of a talker and when I tried reading him this morning while at the dinette table, his mind was cluttered with *things* – geometric objects like cubes and cylinders and pyramids of various sizes that danced and collided into each other, thus multiplying through osmosis. Dizzying to the point

of nausea. Think Disney's *Fantasia*, and add chaos into the mix. I
escaped his interior world with my teeth tense and aching.

Ah! Yes! Back to my own thoughts, my own imagination. Back
to work!

I pulled out my laptop from under the cot – Aly had gotten it
and a few of my other necessities from my apartment in Queens –
and I sat in the 'dining area' to get back to my writing. I lost track
of time as I worked on <u>Symbiote Sight.</u>

I was at a critical moment in my writing:

```
Sarker was unlocking the front door to his
home when he heard an odd noise behind him.
The entity wrapped inside his brain twisted in
warning. Sarker crouched as he turned and readied
```

"Didn't you hear the phone?"

I jumped and gave a shriek, almost knocking over my laptop.

Brian Gainer stood opposite me at the round table. "Aly called."

That was it. Nothing further from him. He stared with his
brown eyes without expression.

I breathed again. "Dad get off all right?" I asked.

"Yes. She stayed with him till he boarded."

While he stood there silently, I took several seconds to consider
what, exactly, Alyson saw in him. To me, 'Bri' had ordinary features,
neutral almost, like a Ken doll. He was simply an ordinary-looking
guy in his early thirties, clean-shaven, with brown hair that hung
messily straight over his forehead, who was maybe an inch taller
than me.

When Aly began dating him (six or more years ago), she told
me he was 'devastatingly handsome' and on another occasion that

he had 'movie-star good looks.' I never saw it. He shared none of my interests so we never had any real connection. End of story.

"Aly's doing a job in Patterson," he said finally. "She's working with a client."

Aly was a computer programmer by formal education. She became a private computer consultant and trouble shooter on her own volition. The work gave her a great deal of independence.

Uncomfortable with Brian peering at me, three-dimensional geometrics swirling in his skull, I said, "Did she say anything else? Anything she'd like me to do?"

"Yes. She said we can go have lunch out if we want to. Alex. Do you want to have lunch out together? I mean, with me?"

"Sure," I answered and smiled. "I didn't realize the time. My stomach's beginning to growl."

"I'll get my coat," he said.

I packed up my laptop and got on my shoes. When Brian came out of the bedroom shrugging on his suede coat, I asked, "Where are we going to eat?"

"I thought maybe, Washington Square? That okay?"

"Sounds great." I hadn't hung around the Village in a couple of years. Not since I stopped dating Susan who was attending NYU. When she graduated Law School, she moved to Nebraska. Or someplace like that.

We could run into some co-eds. I was about to mention that to Brian, looked at him, and decided not to say it aloud. Self-consciously, I touched the bandage on top of my head that Aly had changed this morning. It was little more than a glorified band-aide now and my hair helped to hide it. I looked almost human again.

Brian waited patiently by the door as I got my coat from the walk-in closet.

"Ready," I said, and headed toward him.

Brian nodded and pointed to my corner. "On the phone, Aly said."

"What?"

"Your cane."

"Oh. Yeah. That's right." I thought immediately of what Larry had told me. I should try to look 'fragile.' Stumble around a bit. My metal cane was leaning against the radiator. I got it and tested it against the floor.

That's when it hit me. This could be it. Larry's plan. The Mr. Quiver Mission. My heart flung itself against my coat at the thought. My fingertips tingled as a chill spread through my legs. Walking across the room, I found myself feigning a limp. Brian opened the door and we marched to the elevator, Brian letting me choose our pace.

In the elevator, I casually touched the tab on the flag pin. *And so, it begins. Again.* It occurred to me then that nothing had happened the previous times I had gone out because Dad was with me. Now that he was safely out of the way, Jaime (or whomever) might indeed be seen, if he/she/it is indeed shadowing me. *Thus, the Mission is in play!*

We reached the lobby and headed outside. It was a cool but sunny day for mid-November. Mild enough. On the grounds of the apartment complex, people were sitting on benches and strolling comfortably. When we got onto Broome Street, crowds of people strode by.

I turned to Brian and asked, "Today is Friday, isn't it?"

"Yes. Nice day."

"It is. But so many people out and about. Isn't this a work day?"

"Yes. Still, people do things."

I loved Brian's simple comments. Uncritical. I was sure that was the way he saw the world. People were neither good nor bad. They simply *were*.

Brian was leading me but he remained staunchly by my side as I hobbled along using the cane. I was conscious of the camera lens in my flag pin and walked with forced stiffness, turning slightly right and left to give whoever was watching the camera's monitor a wide view. *Would I see Jaime walking past? How do I catch someone behind me with the camera lens?* I edged close to shop windows and stopped to capture reflections of the street behind us. Only for a moment at a time, though, before moving on. At one point, I stopped beside a broad store front window and nodded at an attractive young mother wheeling a baby carriage and passing us. Self-consciously, I turned the way we had come to sweep the street crowds behind us. My stomach jumped as I recalled what Larry had in mind. Someone could come out of a shop and start arguing with me, an argument that was designed to escalate . . . So many people sauntered through the Village: young, old, marrieds, singles on the make – all types.

We turned north on West Broadway toward Houston Street. There, Brian cut left and slowed his pace to stay with me as we got to MacDougal Street. We walked north along MacDougal. I continued looking into shop windows to see if I could spot anyone who might be tracking us. I wasn't very good at it, hoping that my flag pin lens would pick up what I couldn't see. The mixed food smells coming from multifarious bistros pursued me at every step.

"Did I mention I was hungry?" I said.

"Yes."

"Well, we're walking past lots of eateries. We passed by Saigon Shack, the place that we ordered take-out from the first night I stayed with you. And there's Minetta Tavern across the street. Expensive, I know, but Hemingway, Eugene O'Neill, and Dylan Thomas ate there. It's been awhile since . . ."

"I have something in mind," he said. "My favorite place. Okay?"

"Sure. You're the host."

That made him smile. His pace quickened and I tapped the cane on the pavement faster to keep up. He murmured, "I'm the host."

We approached W. 3rd Street and headed up toward Washington Square Park.

"There it is," said Brian, a note of excitement in his voice. "Across the street."

I saw a shop with an awning and the sign 'Mamoun's Falafel.' After crossing, we found several people seated at tables under the awning while others crowded the entrance. The enticing odors of garlic, tahini sauce, and roasting lamb tantalized me.

We gradually made it inside – the line of customers was short and moved rapidly. The interior was similar to a pizza joint in Queens I frequented, but the lighting was a dull yellow that tossed long shadows on everything, creating an otherworldly atmosphere. Hanging on one brick wall was a wood cut that caught my interest. Written in bold black letters, it read: "Remember from Whence You Came." It made me think of Mom and the car accident four years ago and how my special ability had grown from such accidents. I turned away from the woodcut just as my eyes started to water.

Couples and threes sat at small tables lining both sides of the place and, facing us, was a long hardwood counter behind which several countermen wearing black tee-shirts with a cartoonish image of a mustached man and the words 'Mamoun's Falafel' hustled to take orders. We could see steam rising out of swinging doors from the kitchen way in the back.

"Brian," called out an attractive young woman with long red hair. She stepped from behind the counter dressed in a too small 'Mamoun's Falafel' tee-shirt that clung snugly to her frame above tight blue jeans. She rushed over to us and gave 'my host' a long affectionate hug. Then she stepped back and held his shoulders firmly. "Why haven't you been around lately? It's been too long." Her accent was foreign, and I guessed that perhaps she was Greek. That's how it sounded anyway.

"Bridge tournament," Brian answered, a grin on his face. "And work. Keeping me busy. This is my brother-in-law, Alex."

"Hello." She smiled at me. "Have I seen you in here before?"

"I don't think so," I replied. "But maybe you've read --"

A loud voice called out, "Helena," (pronounced He-LEEN-e). It came from a large dark-complexioned man in the uniform black tee and wearing a red "Mamoun's Falafel' peaked cap, brim backward, standing to one side of the counter. The woman speaking to us jumped and turned to look. The man added, "You've got customers!" He was holding two plates of pita bread and steaming food. "They're waiting!"

"Okay, Benjy," she shouted back. She turned again to Brian and patted his face. "Say goodbye to me before you leave." She sauntered over to Benjy, took the two plates from him and headed to the tables outside.

I noticed that many of the young men watched Helena as she moved. She had lovely swinging hips and pressing breasts beneath her overtly close-fitting tee-shirt. I noted that Brian also was watching her. So was I.

I looked at Brian and said, "You're a popular guy here. Come often?"

He looked at me, a grin on his face. "Whenever I can. The food is superb."

I tried to read him just then but I sensed nothing. *He can't be blocking me, the dimwit! He's simply shut down! Embarrassed, perhaps. That would be his way.*

"Let's put in our order," Brian said, and we went to a scarecrow-thin counterman with curled black hair and a broad grin. "What can I get you?" he asked.

I ordered Shawarma, roasted lamb with a blend of parsley, garlic, and tahini sauce, on pita bread. Brian ordered Baba Ganouj, roasted eggplant. We both ordered drinks, Brian a ginger ale and me an iced tea. "Have a seat," the counterman said with a smile. "Helena will bring it." The fellow must have watched Helena while she was with us. Brian led the way to find seating. I could see an empty table near the entrance.

As we wended our way between customers entering the place, I was roughly pushed aside from behind. My cane scraped the wood floor as I stumbled and Brian caught me. Startled, I turned to see a tall teenager with long black hair shove his way by me with the large backpack he had on.

"Move it!" snapped the youth. He stopped, turned, and glared at me. I picked up from his mind an image of me as a stooped little man with unkempt hair. His imagining dissolved from my view with the reality of his dark face before me. He mumbled, "Slow bastard!"

Brian turned to face him. "Watch it."

The tall kid muttered something unintelligible and continued to stride away. He sat at a table with two other teenage boys. As he dropped his backpack on the floor, he shared a word with them and they all laughed.

I lifted my cane and was ready to storm their table but Brian stepped in my way.

"It's not worth it. Forget the whole thing."

I stared at Brian's noncommittal face and he nodded in a calming manner. Then he guided me to the empty table I had spotted.

I saw Helena coming in our direction and Brian waved at her with a grin. Glancing across the way at the table with the three teenage boys, I saw the one who had shoved me talking loudly to his friends. He pushed his chair back and started getting up. One of the other boys put his hand out to stop him but he roughly jabbed it away. All the while, he kept his eyes on me.

This is it! I thought. *The set up. Larry's behind this. Get ready.*

Brian turned from Helena's approach to look at me. I had jumped in my seat with anticipation. My cane inadvertently hit his leg.

I searched the front of Mamoun's and the street outside the window for anyone recognizable: Larry or Jaime or someone showing an unusual interest in me. Nobody stood out. The kid walked away from his table and came toward us, eyes ablaze.

I strained to pick up any familiar thoughts. "Larry? You out there?"

"What?" asked Brian.

I stared fixedly at him. Shaking my head, I murmured, "I don't think I can avoid getting punched in the face."

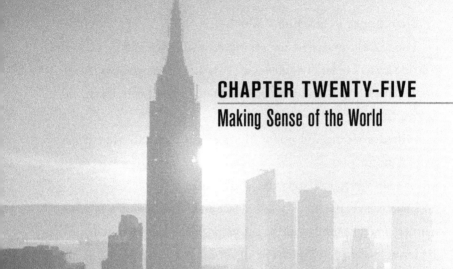

CHAPTER TWENTY-FIVE
Making Sense of the World

I tried to read the teenager as he neared our table. Nothing. He kept his mind shut tight. If he had been hired for this, he wasn't letting on.

Before leaving his two friends at their table, he had taken something out of his backpack. He held it in his clenched hand. I couldn't quite tell what it was.

No weapons, I recalled. *Prime rule. Not even fake ones.*

"Don't worry," Brian told me. He put his hand on my shoulder. "He's just a kid. He won't start anything in a public place like this."

That's exactly where he'll start something. If Larry arranged this.

I looked around anxiously, afraid that Helena might be swept up in the proceedings. She had gone to another table, talking to three seated women, one with a baby carriage. Perhaps they were part of a diversion Larry had planned for. Was Helena part of the plan? Or the three women? I didn't really know.

The teen stood over me. "Heh! You!" the kid snarled. "You him?"

Brian squeezed my shoulder so that it hurt. I shrugged from the pain but his hold kept me from getting out of my chair.

"What do you mean?" I muttered back at the kid.

He lifted the object in his hand. It was a hard-covered book. He showed the back cover with a portrait photo on it. MY portrait photo. From five years ago. Outdoors. Arizona, I think. At a convention out west. It was a low shot of me looking upward, three-quarter face, square-jawed, wire-rimmed glasses, hands on hips, and looking heroically toward the future. Dressed in a Western-style shirt and buckskin vest. An asteroid streaked across the sky above me. The adventurous, far-thinking Alex Brocton.

"This you?" the teen grumbled. "Brocton? You?"

Brian reached out with a fumbling hand. He was clearly trying to distract the kid from doing anything harmful to me. "What you got there?" he asked. "A book?"

"Yeah, chief," the kid said. He turned back to me and showed the cover. "I'm into this, Bro. Evolved Parameters. You this Brocton?"

"Yeah. That's me."

The teen did something unexpected then. Remarkable, even. He smiled. A wide tooth-filled smile. It changed his entire face. Dark eyes were suddenly rounded and admiring. He stood gangly, like a child feeling self-conscious and bashful. The image flowing from his mind was of me as I appeared in a television interview I did three years ago for the Syfy Channel. My hair was neater than I'd ever gotten it myself, face smoothed with make-up, my earnest eyes prominent behind stylish eyeglasses. I looked fantastic.

I couldn't hear the words in the kid's mind, but I knew what I was saying in the thought he projected. My statement had been quoted often in the magazines and at conventions. It became a mantra.

"The wonder of reading science fiction," I recited, allowing myself a grin, "is how it makes sense of the world we have to live in."

"That the jam, Bro," the kid said. "'Wonder of science fiction . . . makes sense of this world.' For real. It grabs me." He knelt and held out his right hand with his fingers partly closed. When I put out mine to shake hands, he clasped it, intertwined my fingers with his, and performed an elaborate handshake that culminated with a butting of knuckles. He stood and smiled broadly as he gestured in a sloppy kind of salute and backed away. "You jammin,' Bro. S'goo ta meet. Keep it real." He stooped again to whisper, "Where your glasses? You look smart wid them on, y'know?"

He returned to his friends, jumping up and down in his chair as he spoke in loud grunts, pointing toward me and to the book he held.

Just then, Helena showed up with our food and Brian fell to it right away. I continued to watch the three teens as they rose from their seats. My young fan looked at me with a dopey grin and made something like a peace sign with his hand. Then they rambled out of the place and disappeared down the street.

"Something, huh!" Brian said, chewing a mouthful of eggplant and pita bread. "Didn't know you were so popular."

"Yeah," I answered, and bit into my sandwich. "Kid didn't apologize for knocking into me. Didn't tell me his name. Worst of all --" I took a gulp of my drink.

"What?"

"He didn't bother to ask for my autograph."

Brian shook his head. "That's just the way teenagers are these days."

Sure. That meant the kid was not part of the plan. He wasn't pretending.

I sat there chewing my lamb glumly. I was sorely disappointed.

CHAPTER TWENTY-SIX
The Redoubtable Mr. Gainer

*T*hat wasn't it! Damn! *That tall teenager would've been so easy. If it had been a set-up, I wouldn't have really gotten a punch in the face. And then it would've been over. We'd have our guy. Mister Fucking Quiver!*

"Stupid idea anyway!" I mumbled to myself.

Brian looked at me. "What was that?"

"Nothing," I said. *How could you know anything about it, Bri?* "Just a tad annoyed. That didn't go as expected."

"Oh. Well, kids don't care about things like keeping autographs of famous people. Who knows what they care about these days?"

You really are a bit dim, Brian. It's this stupid plan of Larry Coates!

I watched glumly as Brian finished the last of his sandwich and looked at his watch. A light seemed to go off in his head – not that I saw anything. "It seems to me you should be very pleased," he said.

"Why?"

"You're recognized! You've got fans who come up to you on the street. And . . . even wayward kids like that are reading! Not just books, but YOU. They're reading your novels. Something to be proud of. What time do you have?"

"Huh?" I looked at my watch. "One-fifteen. Why?"

"Would you like to come with me to Washington Square Park?"

"I thought that's where we were going."

"Yes, but I mean right now. Something I want to see."

"Sure. I'm ready."

Brian led as we walked up West 3rd Street to Washington Square South. I heard the distinct sound of live guitar music playing some modern version of an old folk song. I felt for the flag pin on my coat lapel and found the tab still down. The camera was working, recording what I was seeing and presumably getting our voices as well. That whole exchange with the teenage fan at Mamoun's was listened to by somebody monitoring it.

We stepped into that picturesque scene that was Washington Square Park. Music from a flute and steel drums sliced the air with semi-classical sounds in counterpoint to the continuing folk song of the guitar. People strolled along the walkways, every age represented, though to my mind, there were numerous pairs and groups of young women, many who could be students at NYU.

Let me hear you! Jaime, are you around? Larry, are you near enough for me to hear your thoughts? Anyone? Anyone who's in on Larry's plan? Are you around? Let me hear.

Maybe I should pull out my cell phone and check in with Larry. I brushed hard against an old man walking with a wooden cane. He glared at me as he went on. *No, you ass! Any of these people could be in on it, observing my every move. Just go with it.*

I looked into the faces of people walking by. I turned and scanned those coming up behind us. Anxious to get on with the plan – if this was the right time for it to take place -- I concentrated on receiving other people's mental images. It was hard. I had limits and picking up the imaginings of strangers had become much more difficult since I took that beating in the hotel. Maybe I was really beginning to lose my ability!

We walked by the small dog run where a terrier was excitedly barking and prancing around a lazy spaniel that studied the terrier with half-open eyes, clearly bored. A few of the dog owners holding leashes in their hands stood by inside the fence watching their wards. I stopped a moment – Brian caught himself a couple of yards ahead and backtracked to me – I stood admiring the circular fountain and the Washington Arch beyond it. *God! It has been a long time!*

I saw the drummer and flute player standing in front of the fountain, crowds gathering around them to listen. The steel drum player was a young woman with long hair the color of straw and the flute player was a gray-bearded man who appeared to have transported out of the sixties. I was entranced by the familiar melody of a recent rock opera they had begun playing. A guitarist on the far side of the fountain joined in, keeping harmony.

There. On the bench. A comely young lady in a blue overcoat and faded jeans watched me curiously. I stepped closer to her bench just as Brian reached me. The girl (in her early twenties, I thought), brushed back her hair and gave me a smile. I did my best to ignore Brian as I made eye contact with the girl. *What are you thinking?* I wondered. *Say something good to me.*

"Hello," she murmured. Her voice was soft flame. "I like the strength you show in your walk. Even with that cane." She smiled then, and I knew she meant what she said. Had she said those words because I influenced her in some way?

"This way," Brian said, and looked at his watch. "He's already begun."

"Who?"

"You'll see, Alex. This is something really good."

Brian took me by the elbow and hurried me along. I tried for a final glance of the girl on the bench. Had she suddenly frowned and touched her forehead in pain? I caught a brief glimpse of her movement before people parading by blocked my view; that pained look had happened to Detective Ambrose and Nurse Renee. But that had happened only after I questioned them out loud. Here, I hadn't spoken. Could I have reached into this young woman's mind and elicited her response? How is that possible?

I'd never seen Brian so impatient. He released his hold on my elbow but he gestured and looked back at me several times to rush me on. As we paced quickly, my metal cane rapidly striking the walkway, I dared to probe his mind. The dancing geometrics in his imagining were changing. Twirling cubes and triangles transformed into two black-armored horsemen and a man in black ecclesiastical robes facing three white-armored foot soldiers protecting a white-cloaked woman with a coronet on her head. And then I knew.

The chess district was near Thompson Street at the southwest edge of Washington Square Park. Players sat on benches in stolid concentration moving chess pieces on boards built on top of stone tables. Devotees and passing idlers stood watching the games, occasionally saying a few words to their comrades beside them. The players sat stiffly, hardly moving at all until, here and there, an individual player would jettison forward with sudden vigor to move a piece. Cutting the still air of a sudden, a player would cry out "Check," and, very occasionally but inevitably, the sharp call "Checkmate."

Bri led me to that.

We stood by a table where a sandy-haired man with a bushy mustache and a cherry-wood pipe in his mouth played against a lanky kid wearing an NYU jacket. The college kid had much fewer chess pieces than the pipe smoker. Several thin groups of onlookers milled around to watch several different chess games at adjacent tables but a good half-dozen stayed steadfastly by the pipe smoker's table.

"Bri," called out the pipe smoker, sitting back to wait for the kid's next move. "Glad you made it. Got time to play?"

"You bet!" said Brian. "This time, Karl, I don't plan to lose."

Karl laughed. "You know, neither do I."

I was familiar with the basic moves of chess and played it when I was a teenager in high school. I just never got into the game and, consequently, wasn't very good at it. But I could still follow the play.

The kid pointedly picked up his white knight and placed it sharply two squares and over to confront the black king.

"Check," he said.

Karl captured the knight with a rook. The kid placed a pawn one space closer to Karl's side of the board, a rather ineffectual move. Karl slid his bishop diagonally toward the kid's end where it joined several of his own pieces, including his queen. He paused as he held onto his bishop, then removed his hand and sat back. "Checkmate."

The kid examined the board carefully, then reached out and knocked over his king. Shaking his head, he murmured, "Thanks for the game." He quickly got up and headed out of the park.

Taking his pipe out of his mouth, Karl scanned the faces of our little group. "Who's next?"

Brian grinned broadly, his mind filled with images of the white cloaked king wielding his sword and two white knights on horseback galloping to protect their queen. I could see that I was about to be treated to a match between Karl and the redoubtable Brian Gainer.

"I am," said a woman wearing a brown Stetson and dark glasses. She sat on the bench opposite Karl and immediately began setting up the white chess pieces. "I've been waiting here longer than anybody else." She eyed the onlookers around her, making a point of settling her look on Brian beside me. "All right?"

Brian looked at her, then at Karl. "Okay with me. Karl?"

"Sure," he said. "She's been standing here for a long time." He looked at her as he set up his own pieces. He smiled. "This may not take long."

Her voice strident, the woman said, "You may be surprised."

She began by moving queen's pawn one space. Karl moved knight's pawn forward. The play proceeded briskly from there.

Have I seen this woman before? Something familiar about her.

I felt a warmth of eagerness flowing from her but little else. She was dressed in a brown corduroy jacket and matching pants, flat-heeled shoes, heavy knit sweater, wool scarf around her neck, and the aforesaid Stetson cowboy hat and large dark glasses that hid much of her face. I had the odd feeling that she wasn't dressed in her usual clothes. I know, I know! I had nothing to go on. But the feeling was strong. It was as if she was wearing a costume.

She looks damn familiar!

I whispered to Brian, "Have you seen her here before?"

"No," he answered, looking at me. "Why? Do you know her?"

"No. I don't know. I don't think so."

"Check," came from the woman.

Karl was surprised. At least, that was what I sensed in him, though I probably could have read it in his face. It was early in the game and he reviewed the chess pieces carefully. Her white knight threatened his black king. Karl took the knight with his bishop and their play continued. I could feel a sudden and mounting tension building in Karl.

I can't get too absorbed in this game, I knew. *I'm a pawn in a much larger game.*

Stepping back from the small group of seven or eight people watching the chess players, I allowed for the flag pin camera to scan the park while I also gazed around. *There! Sitting at the fountain! Could that be Jaime?* It was a heavy-set man, hair very dark. Too far to tell! He could have been Jaime but at that distance he could've been anybody. I just *wanted* it to be Jaime.

A fragmentary glimmer of myself flashed through my mind from someone's thought: Me, dressed as I was but close up and wearing my glasses!

I twisted around to catch the one who radiated that image. No, it wasn't from that heavy-set man. He got up and walked toward the Arch and disappeared on the other side. I spotted the same guitarist we had heard when we entered the park; he was strumming his guitar as he headed toward the Arch also. Was he following the heavy-set man? Probably not. More likely, it was my sense of urgency and a bit of paranoia speaking.

Then the flash of image came again: corrected – me without my glasses!

Who are you? Where are you?

"Check!"

The woman facing Karl, again. She had gotten a pawn through, undetected, while Karl had warily engaged and avoided her higher level pieces. He took her pawn with his king, moving it into the second row – and perhaps into exposure.

She took her Stetson off, placed it beside her on the bench, and then leaned forward to study the board. I saw that she had blonde hair tightly bound and streaked with gray. She took off her sunglasses and cupped her chin in her hand. Her cheeks were deeply lined. I couldn't see her eyes. But her profile was *very* familiar.

The glimpse of me again in someone's mind: Lying in a hospital bed, wearing my glasses. *Yes!* I realized. *I know you! You came to the hospital in Philly. Tell me!*

"Yes," she said, aloud. Everyone heard her, including Brian. I knew for a certainty then.

Detective Daugherty! It's you!

"Yes," she said, her eyes on the chess pieces. "It's me." She moved her queen across the board. A daring move. "Check."

I wondered if Detective Ambrose was also here. *No! Not the time nor the place to start the detective talking. Did Larry . . . No! No questions! Not right now, anyway.*

Karl took a long time examining the board. I virtually smelled his fear and couldn't help my wry smile. Yes! Fear does smell. It smells like week-old dead fish!

He moved his king one space back, held onto the piece, comprehending that his one remaining rook was already in play and therefore unusable for castling. He released his hold of the king. Even I could see that Daugherty would now have him on the run.

Daugherty moved her bishop so that it had one space between it and Karl's black king on the diagonal. She called, "Check."

Karl took her bishop with his queen. A dangerous move and I felt his regret.

"Look at that," Brian whispered to me. "Karl's not doing so well."

Daugherty went for the opening. She captured Karl's queen with a rook. The crowd around us muttered sounds of disappointment. I saw Karl's distress -- but then, most of the onlookers did also.

"I think she's going to beat him," Brian told me.

"WHERE DO YOU THINK YOU'RE GOING?"

The sharp aggressive shout disrupted everything. The players stopped their game and turned toward Washington Square South, as did all of us. Stunned, we watched as a man chased a young girl up the path in our direction.

The girl was about eighteen, wearing a dark red coat and blue jeans, and the man, an unshaven rough-looking guy, was dressed in a leather jacket, black pants, and boots.

"Get back here!" shouted the leather-jacketed man.

He grabbed her by the arm and pulled her painfully toward him. "You ain't going nowhere!"

"Leave me alone!" cried the girl, pulling her arm free of his grasp and storming up the pathway.

The girl rushed right at me. I could see a large bruise around her right eye and a cut on her lip. Her gaze fell on me.

"Look out!" she cried as she came within inches of me. She pushed me and I stumbled back, dropping my cane noisily. Brian caught me before I could fall. As he handed back my cane, I touched the thick bandage partially hidden in my scalp.

Perfect! I look the part of a fragile man, just as Larry had suggested. And I'm getting some attention. If Jaime is around, he'd take notice.

Leather jacket held the girl in a painful grip and slapped her across the face. "I told you not to go out!" he shouted. "Who're you going to see? Huh? Who?"

I looked into their faces. Was this real? *God! That guy's damn furious! I see the sweat dripping from his hair.* Were they such good actors that I couldn't sense they were pretending? *That girl's fear isn't put on! I see the pain in her eyes.* Or were they so caught up in the emotions that he felt his rage and she was immersed in fright? I felt the quickening thump in my chest and an increasing unease. This *felt* real to me. That was what mattered.

The girl hit him hard in the face and got away from him again.

People around us stood and watched, stunned. Some of the onlookers quickly left the area but others gathered out of curiosity. I heard muttered complaints of "Call 911," and "Crazy people in New York!" Chess players got up and stood by. Karl and Daugherty both rose, Karl calling out, "What the hell's going on?"

"Move back, Alex," Brian said. "This has nothing to do with you."

Damnit, Brian! This has everything to do with me! I'm the reason this is happening! Me! My doing!

As the leather-jacketed guy tried to grab the girl by her shoulders, she twisted away and turned back toward us. It was inevitable that she would head back to me.

"Alex?" the girl asked, more as confirmation than to ask my aid. I blinked – surprised more than to confirm who I was. But that was enough. That was what the leather-jacketed guy needed. He strode up to us at Mach Four.

He was close enough that I saw his slickly moist whiskers and chin hair. His dark eyes glared with intensity. "What the hell you lookin' at?" he growled.

Brian stepped between the guy and me. "He's not looking at anything," he said.

The guy stared straight at me but answered Brian by pushing him aside. "No one's talkin' to you." To me: "You know Bethany? You know my girl?" Then, to Bethany, "This the guy? You came out for him?"

"I . . ." I began, trying to think of something not too clever. "I don't know this --"

"Shaddup, you! Bethy, baby. This the one?"

"I went out for a walk!" the girl cried. "I wasn't going to see anyone. Why can't I go out when I want to, Greg?"

"Then . . . Then why'd you run from me? Heh? Why'd you do that?"

"'Cause you scared the shit out of me! That's why, you prick!"

"You should listen to her," I said, trying to sound reasonable. Larry *had* told me I should step up when the action got started.

"You!" Greg shouted. He grabbed me by my coat collar and the flag pin made a feedback sound – too low for anybody else to hear.

He pulled me bodily to one side. My cane dropped out of my hand again. Greg raised a fist, drawing his elbow well back. I was going to be clobbered after all.

"No! Stop!" said Brian, coming forward, arms outstretched. Not fast enough.

Greg slammed his fist across my ear, more lightly than I expected. Someone bigger than Brian or Greg – or me – shoved Brian aside. I had the briefest of glances at him: large far-apart eyes, black shaggy hair, meaty face. It was Jaime!

Jaime lunged into Greg, throwing him hard to the ground. He started punching Greg. Hell, he never stopped punching him! And then someone grabbed Jaime's thick neck from behind, put him in a stranglehold, dragged him off Greg, and rolled him onto the ground. Greg's face was bruised and bloody.

I shook as I leaned against a bench. Shock, I suppose. Breathless, I stood by, feeling useless. It was Brian lying on top of Jaime. Brian who stepped in to help.

"Stay there!" demanded a stern female voice. Detective Daugherty stood over the three men, holding a revolver directly above Jaime's ear. Six pairs of eyes gaped up at her, at the gun in her hand. "Don't get up! Just stay where you are, all of you!"

Shaken and drawing in deep breaths, I heard a middle-aged woman nearby say: "It's all so surreal!"

The scene was real, all right. Nothing surreal about it. This was New York. Three hard-breathing men were sprawled on the dirt and grass: the bloody-faced Greg, the open-mouthed Jaime, and my brother-in-law, smiling at the crowd. The redoubtable Mr. Gainer.

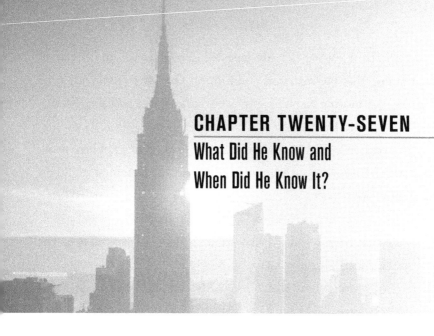

CHAPTER TWENTY-SEVEN
What Did He Know and When Did He Know It?

"**A**RE YOU CRAZY? Why'd you do a thing like that?"

"It seemed like the right thing to do."

"I've never heard anything so ridiculous! You might've been killed!"

"Oh, I don't think so. Do you, Alex?"

Up until then, I had been a disinterested observer, taking a breath and being somewhat amused by the verbal conflict. Up until then.

"Well, uh, no. That doesn't seem likely, Bri. Alyson."

The three of us sat around the little dinette table in Aly and Brian's apartment. It was after 9:00 at night and we were hungry. Brian and I spent hours with the police, being questioned and giving our statements. When Aly came to get us – I had phoned her -- we picked up Chinese take-out. On the way home, all Aly would say to us is, "We'll talk about it later!" It was most unlike her. I tried to sense her thinking but her mind was a deeply dark void that ached like a jagged wound.

"Why'd you do it?" Aly repeated. "What made you decide to jump on that big man and pull him off the other guy? Wasn't the other guy beating up on his girlfriend?" She looked accusingly at me. "That's what Alex said."

"Yes, well, the big guy seemed the greater danger. There was a chance that he'd punch out others around us. I thought he might go after Alex."

Aly gave me a hard stare. "Why would he go after Alex?"

"After the guy and girl showed up, things just seemed to center around Alex."

"Why do you say that?" asked Aly, looking from me to Brian and back again. "Alex?"

"Well, Aly," I said, "I kind of recognized --"

"I saw that something else was going on," Brian jumped in. "Things didn't fit."

It was my turn to stare, confounded by my brother-in-law. "What do you mean: 'things didn't fit'?"

"Let me think. Well, the way that girl circled around us. That didn't seem normal. Someone that afraid would continue running right out of the park."

I felt an untoward sensation in watching the animated face of my brother-in-law. This was new. I'd never seen this side of him. What was it? What was this thing I saw in Brian?

"Some other things I noticed," he went on. "When she got close to us, that bruise mark around her eye seemed to get smudged – like make-up. And I was sure she called your name."

Aly stared at him. "So, what are you saying? The girl wasn't really beaten up? That she knew Alex?" She turned to me. "Do you know that girl?"

"No. Really. I never saw her before."

"Yes, and the guy," Bri said, "pulled that punch so that it barely touched you. I saw it because I was right next to you, but anyone standing at a distance would think it was a direct hit. It wasn't, was it, Alex?"

Checkmate.

He caught me. Brian had me by the balls and I had to wonder if he knew what he was saying or was simply making guesses. To put it another way; did Brian know that I was an integral part of a real-life chess game?

"Okay, Bri. When did you figure it out?"

Aly asked, "Figure what out?"

"The way you were gyrating down the street," he said. "Staying close to shop windows to look at reflections. Turning around to view people behind us. What is it? A camera? What, was it that flag pin you wore so conspicuously on your coat? Strange place for it."

Shit! And I always thought him a dull-minded schlemiel!

"Larry gave me that camera to wear whenever I went out. It was Larry's plan."

"Larry's plan for WHAT?" asked Aly.

"To find the big man with the far apart eyes. The guy's been watching me for years. He sent me a note saying so, that he would protect me. He signed it 'Mr. Quiver.' Aly, I told you all that at the convention, the night you visited."

"Yes, I remember," Aly said. "You were talking about Uncle George making hand shadows. He created 'Mr. Quiver.' But I thought that big man calling himself Mr. Quiver intended to be your protector. Why would he want to hurt you?"

"He wasn't going to hurt me," I said. "Brian's wrong about that. Larry arranged for that leather-jacketed guy and the girl to start a fight around me so that the big guy would try to rescue me."

"THAT was Larry's plan? Larry cooked up that ridiculous idea?"

"And the lady," Brian said with a nod of his head.

Aly asked, "What lady?"

"The lady that sat down at the chess table and began beating the pants off of my friend Karl. The one with the gun." He turned to me and pointed his finger. "You asked me if I'd seen her before. You acted like you were startled when you saw her. Was that for real?"

"Yes, it was. I had no idea Daugherty would show up. Larry told me that the police wouldn't be involved officially. But he said that didn't mean there wouldn't be police around."

"So you honestly didn't know she'd be there?"

Aly interrupted: "Who is this woman you're talking about?"

"Detective Daugherty," I said. "She was one of the two detectives who came to see me at the hospital."

"A police detective? From Philadelphia? What did they want with you in the hospital?"

"They questioned me about the death of Dennis Leibowitz."

"So," Aly said, "this plan of Larry's was to capture the man who killed that cracked fan of yours at the convention? That's what it was about?"

"Yes," I answered cautiously. I didn't think it needed spelling out to this extent.

"And you deliberately made yourself a target of this killer? And put my husband in harm's way?"

"Well . . ."

"You put people in danger to capture your Mr. Quiver? Are you shitting me?"

"It was the only way to --"

"I've heard enough! Alex! I'm putting my foot down."

I asked, "What are you going to do?"

"I'm not letting the two of you get together and go off on your own ever again! I won't leave you two boys alone to pull such antics."

Stunned, Brian and I looked at each other.

"YOU HEAR ME?"

In unison, we said, "Yes. We hear you."

CHAPTER TWENTY-EIGHT
Case Closed

His name was James Everett. He was a computer programmer working at Valastro Interactives Corporation. He was thirty-four years old. Height: six feet five inches. Weight: two hundred and ten pounds. Place of residence: 34 Woodland Place, Haverstraw, New York. Criminal Record: None.

Larry Coates called me from the police precinct that same night to give me this basic information about the man we knew as Jaime. Larry would call again as soon as he learned anything further.

I waited.

"Hello, Alex?" The call came about twenty-five minutes past midnight. Aly and Brian were already in their bedroom, presumably asleep. "This is Larry Coates."

I smiled. Obvious as always, he *would* identify himself like that. I half expected him to add: 'Your friend, the lawyer.'

"Yes, Larry. I know. So, what's the story?"

"Can you come down tomorrow morning at ten o'clock? It's a mess down here but they'll give you a few minutes with James Everett. Supervised, of course."

"Sure. Where do I go?"

"Manhattan Central Booking."

"Okay. Where's that?"

"100 Centre Street. Take a cab. You sure you lived in New York all your life?"

"Yeah, Larry. I just never had occasion to visit the City jails before."

"Well, it's an experience. Will you be able to make it tomorrow?

"Yes, I'll be there. Where do I meet you?"

"Security will direct you after you've been screened. They'll have a visitor's pass waiting for you. I don't know if I'll see you before you go in for your interview but I can't be with you when you talk to Everett anyway. I have no standing there. It's their ballgame now. NYPD.

"Now, listen. They won't let you speak to him alone. You'll probably be in a conference room with a court-appointed attorney for Everett and at least two police officers. One of them will be a Sergeant William Mataro. He's the officer in charge. It's likely there will be others witnessing your meeting from an observation room. Do you understand?"

"Sure do. I'll be circumspect in what I say."

"Yes. Be circumspect. Be *very* circumspect."

I liked Larry's sense of humor. When I got off the phone, I was nervous as hell about the meeting. Scared out of my mind, actually. But I laughed at Larry's words nevertheless.

The next morning moved like a dream. Like a nightmarish half-slumber that took me by taxi through narrowing litter-strewn streets to dingy-looking buildings, and thence, by foot, carried me in waves through long lines of disconsolate people in periods of painful slowness; only to be caught up in a sudden rush under guard by security on each side of me along immense deserted corridors, handed over from one heavily armed troop of uniformed officers to another.

100 Centre Street was a vast complex of monolithic structures, of which Central Booking was merely one. As I was led through long passages and entranceways, I had the impression that I traveled from one dismal building into another, until I found myself in a sanitized environment which, I saw by way of a hallway sign, was Manhattan Detention.

Not only was I lost in this jumbled maze of security exchanges and concrete, I knew with all certainty that I was trapped.

I was brought to a large office space that was alive with both women and men, some in uniform but others in business attire, working at desks on computers and phones, a few in animated conversation with one another.

"Mr. Brocton?" said a tall slender man in police uniform, unsmiling, peering at me with deeply-lined piercing eyes. He noted my using a metal cane silently and shook my hand with a firm grip. "I'm Sergeant Mataro. This way, please."

He led me from the office down a long well-lit corridor to a door that opened on a narrow rectangular-shaped room with a large window facing another room, one that was dimly lit. In the narrow room I entered, a row of hard wooden chairs lined the center space where observers could watch the next room through the window.

Two men stood waiting in this viewing room, one in a black business suit and the other in a police uniform. They were introduced to me as Mr. Tilden, court-appointed attorney for James Everett, and Officer Madden, who would be recording our interview. Mr. Tilden shook my hand and murmured hello. He eyed me quizzically, eyebrows raised, as if wondering why I was there. Madden didn't look at me but gave a brief wave. He stood checking a video camera and audio device mounted on a console on the far right of the window.

"We'll remain here," Mataro said, "until Mr. Everett enters and is seated at the conference table. Once he's settled, I will accompany you and Mr. Tilden into that room. Don't say anything until I finish with what I have to say. It will all be recorded. When there, follow my directions to the letter. Is that clear?"

"Yes, sir."

Mataro gestured for me to take one of the chairs but I was too nervous to sit. "I'd rather stand," I told him, and clacked my cane on the floor as I walked closer to the window. The one door in the next room opened and the lights suddenly came up, making the room very bright. There was a long metallic conference table and six metal chairs – three on each side – and both table and chairs were bolted to the floor. No wayward suspect was going to start throwing furniture around in that room.

A uniformed police officer entered, looked over the room, and let in two other uniformed men holding onto the arms of a large man by his shirtsleeves. They had this third man sit in the middle chair at the conference table facing the window. I saw then that he was handcuffed.

The officer who first entered the conference room left and the remaining two stood on either side of the seated man.

I looked the man over. He didn't seem very threatening or imposing. It was Jaime, though. James Everett. He was unshaven and his eyes were deeply lined and red rimmed. His shirt was wrinkled as if he had slept in his clothes, if he had slept at all. Although he was a tall man, he now appeared to be shrunken and hunched over. He kept his eyes fixed on his handcuffed hands, never once looking around at the officers nor the large window. I was pretty certain by then that on his side it was a mirror.

"This way, please," Mataro said, and I followed Mr. Tilden the attorney out the door.

In the conference room, Tilden sat beside Jaime, and Mataro directed me to sit across from Jaime. I hung my cane over the back of my chair. Mataro stood at the head of the table so that the video would pick him up only in profile. From where I sat, I realized that the way the camera had been angled on the unseen side of the mirror, it would have an unobstructed view of Jaime.

Sergeant Mataro said a few words that set the date and time and who was present for the interview. "At the request of Mr. James Everett, this interview has been agreed to by all parties." Mataro turned to me. "You may begin."

My throat seemed to close and I struggled for breath. This was it. All my questions would now be answered. *Be circumspect.* For somebody else, with these witnesses and the video camera rolling, how could my questions be fully answered? Well, I was confident about that. Through my unique ability. And Jaime knew that. *Be circumspect.*

"I understand," I began, "that you confessed to killing Dennis Leibowitz?"

He didn't look at me; his eyes remained on his hands. "Yes." The word came out scratchy and not quite human. I tried to remember how his voice sounded and found myself wondering if I had ever heard him speak. This was Jaime but he was a stranger to me. I sought an inner voice coming from him. Not words but some kind of fancied thought. *Can I reach you?*

"Did you know that Dennis planned to attack me?"

Billowing dark-gray fog swelling upward. My face rising from it. *That's from him! I got into his mind!*

"Yes," Jaime said. Eyes still on his hands.

"How did you know?"

"I was there, at Levinson's Bookshop." His voice grew recognizably human. He had timbre and inflection, anyway. He was becoming less of a stranger to me. "Saw the argument," he continued. "Didn't trust him." His eyes still lowered.

And I saw Dennis through Jaime's eyes. Saw events skip along like badly edited newsreel footage. Dennis getting into my apartment. Taking my Infinity Award. Hiding it in his luggage. Bringing it along to the hotel in Philly. Pulling the hotel fire alarm. And the events that followed – from a quite different viewpoint than I remembered them.

"When he attacked me, where were you? What did you do?"

At my question, Mr. Tilden reached out to touch my sleeve, then thought better of it. He looked at me, eyebrows raised. I realized then that this was Tilden's method of eliciting responses, this querulous mannerism. I stared back until he gave a slight shrug.

I couldn't read Tilden; he was still a stranger to me. Besides, I had been concentrating on Jaime – giving him my full attention.

"I followed the two of you," Jaime said. "I listened outside the door to his room." Eyes still lowered.

"How did you get in?"

He raised his head and looked at me. His far-apart eyes, swollen with exhaustion, stared intensely.

I felt a shiver down my back.

"You let me in," he replied.

Funny. I didn't remember that at all. When I was trying to reach the handle of the door, Dennis was busy bashing my noggin in with my award. I was pretty damned sure I hadn't made it to the door. Unless –

"Was there anyone with you?" I asked.

"No." Intense eyes glaring.

Jaime turned his gaze on Mr. Tilden, then Sergeant Mataro, then the mirror. *He's avoiding my probing!*

NO! The syllable erupted out of his mind. He turned back to me, his eyes piercing and searching. Then the floodgates opened!

A female hiding in the hotel room's bathroom. Her face blank. No mouth, no eyes, no features whatsoever. Blank. She knelt low. Peering out from behind the partially open door. I saw she wore pants and long sleeves. I tried to zero in on her sleeves, but -- a shadow of movement as she backed away further.

Who is she?

"I said nobody!" he cried out.

"What was that?" Tilden asked, so startling was Jaime's shout. "Was there someone else?"

Jaime turned to him and eased back on his shoulders. "I worked alone."

My contact was suddenly broken. I couldn't find Jaime's thoughts. Not a touch.

"I think --" Tilden began, "we'd better end this interview so I may confer --"

Sergeant Mataro called out, "This interview is over!"

The uniformed officers on either side of Jaime helped him up. He once again lowered his gaze.

"Hold on!" I called out. My stomach churned and I was choked with staggering disappointment. I raised my voice to a near-shout, addressing Jaime. "Tell me why! Why do this whole thing? Why were you watching?"

He glared at me and I saw it in his mind. A deep blood red cloud billowing toward me. I felt it. Suffocating me. I found myself fighting for air.

There it was. A living image coalescing out of that angry blood red miasma – the image of him as a nine-year old holding my three-year old self in a tight headlock above the concrete floor of an outdoor wading pool. I saw it as Jaime saw it. He was looking down at my child face. Slowly, my limbs grew lax and I stopped breathing. I felt his hatred. Hatred for me. His childish petulance unrestrained!

Why me? Tell me.

In the real world, the two uniformed men were pulling Jaime away from the table and he struggled against them. Mataro rushed around the table to grab him and help drag him out. Tilden was calling out "Don't say anything!"

Leaping to my feet, I found my legs shaking. My cane fell off the back of the chair and clacked loudly on the floor. I was at a loss. *Why? Why start this whole thing?*

And then he sent the answer. In my mind I saw the man with far apart dark eyes, black tousled hair, leaning over me beside the pool. The resemblance to Jaime was clear. Jaime looked very much like that man, his father.

And then another image. A young woman, round-faced and smiling, brown hair hanging wildly in every direction. It was Mom. *Why her? What do you know about Mom?*

His father – Jaime's father – held Mom in his arms. Caressed her, kissed her softly on her cheek.

My mother. His father.

The image popped like a burst bubble.

Back to the interview room: Jaime, still resisting the three men on him, glared at me, his eyes burning into me. Then he resisted no longer. He let them drag him out. Mataro nodded solemnly at me and left the room. Mr. Tilden followed. For several minutes I was alone. Momentarily trapped.

No more images. I couldn't reach him.

Two police officers I hadn't seen before entered and guided me out of the room and out of the building, whisking me outside as if my consciousness were concluding a bad dream. A very bad dream.

It was drizzling outside and I walked the narrow streets looking for a cab.

I knew that Mom had an affair with his father. But why was Jaime thinking about my mother just then? What did he want to convey to me?

The question was unanswered and I ached to know.

CHAPTER TWENTY-NINE
Get Down on the Floor!

I glanced at him as we walked and said, "Someone *was* hurt in that plan of yours, Larry."

"Who?"

"That young actor you got. The tough-looking guy in the leather jacket. It looked like his face was bashed in pretty badly."

"Oh. Phil? He's not an actor."

"No? Who is he?"

"Phil's an NYPD detective. He's the one I told you about. I pay him to help me out sometimes."

"So, he's not angry about the mess you got him into? Getting beaten up?"

"You kiddin'? The scratches on his face give him bragging rights. The precinct lieutenant is putting him in for a commendation for helping to capture James Everett."

"Really? So, he's okay?"

"Of course. In fact, that's why I've got to stop at the bank first before we go to lunch. Phil sometimes asks that I send him a cashier's check for his work. This job, especially. He took it on the sly. After all, he's not with actor's equity."

It was the first day of December and a fresh layer of snow covered the street. Larry and I walked through slush and semi-clear sidewalks on Third Avenue. The upper Eastside. It was a relief not to be using my cane as we sloshed south toward an eatery Larry picked out.

"Okay," I said, "so what have you heard about Jaime's arraignment in Philly?"

"A trial date has been set for January. Detective Daugherty is being very close-mouthed about it."

"What about Daugherty? How'd you first connect with her and get her to come to New York?"

Larry gave me a grin. "You gave me the name in the hospital. Remember? It happened that I reached her by phone first instead of her partner, Ambrose. Besides, it turns out she's one of the most senior police detectives there. When I explained how we intended to get Jaime out in the open, she wanted in. So she took some time off and vacationed in sunny New York City."

"In November?"

"Well, she's senior enough that no one bothered to question her about it. I understand she's a good chess player, too."

"Yeah. She's good. So what happens now? What do I have to do?"

"She told me that you won't have to go to Philly and testify. The D.A. there has accepted your deposition concerning Dennis Leibowitz's attack on you. So, that's that. Anything else?"

"What's going to happen to Jaime?"

"Don't know. Depends on what the D.A. wants. And how the jury finds. I suppose he'll have to serve some time. But no one can get away from the basic truth that he saved your life. If he had only stayed with you and called the police, he might not have been held culpable in Leibowitz's death."

But what about the woman in the room with Dennis? Daugherty knows there was someone else. That could speak to intent on Jaime's part. Some plan to entrap Dennis, or so it would seem. Should I tell Larry about that? Well? Should I?

"Here's my bank," Larry said. "It'll take a minute. Want to wait outside?"

"No. It's cold. I'll go in with you. That okay?"

"Why not?"

He tried the door and found it locked. I looked at my watch. Twelve-seventeen. That seemed a bit odd.

Larry turned to me. "Lunch hour," he said, and smiled. "Must be short of tellers. Why don't we go to lunch and come back --"

The door was pushed out and a good-looking man with neatly-trimmed brown hair leaned toward us. He was dressed in a dark gray business suit, striped blue-gray tie, and unbuttoned tan overcoat. Dark glasses obscured his eyes.

"Come on in, fellas. Didn't mean to keep you." He beamed widely and allowed us to pass. He placed a hand-printed 'Temporarily Closed' sign on the outer door. "We're doing some renovations today."

The bank was quiet. People stood silently, staring at us. A small spread of humanity actually. At a quick count, five women of varying sizes, dress, and ages, and seven men, three in business suits and the others in a variety of overcoats, hats, and slacks. Bank tellers, three, I think, stood behind their respective glass-enclosed counters.

"Actually," said the handsome man in the suit who let us in, "we're just beginning our renovations."

"This way, gentlemen," said another young-looking man in dark glasses, dressed in the exact same fashion as the man who let us in. "No sudden moves, please."

Something's not right, I realized.

Larry turned to the one behind us. "What's up? You two --?"

The second man had stepped from the center of the bank floor. Incongruously, he was holding odd-looking bagpipes in his hands. No, not bagpipes. It was a monstrous stick-like insect with a pointy proboscis. No, not that either. Something worse. Something hideous. Something dangerous. To me, it looked like a short hollowed-out metal cane with branches protruding from it. But by then I knew it for what it was: an ugly foreign-made rapid-firing gun. The kind I've seen only in spy thrillers in the movies. And this second well-dressed young man with dark glasses held it casually, his finger clearly on the trigger, aimed at Larry and me.

Larry expelled a breath. "You're fuckin' kidding me."

Where'd Larry get his balls? Mine had turned to lead. I couldn't feel my legs.

"Move in," the first guy, directly behind us, said.

I moved like an automaton, feeling rivets and washers and screws falling out of mechanical joints in my lower extremities. To put it another way, my knees were turning to soft putty. Still, I imitated Larry as best I could as we made our way toward the other customers.

"Everybody," the second man said, brandishing the weapon, "get down on the floor. Face down. Do it!" The demand was spoken sternly but not shouted.

I slapped the floor hard and winced with pain. I was a mere two seconds ahead of everybody else.

His head next to mine, Larry whispered, "Couldn't you read their minds, Alex? Why didn't you know before we got --"

"No talking," our guy said. Glancing up, I saw that he held a wide-barreled pistol that looked like it was made of white ceramic material.

I don't think it's a toy gun. High tech stuff. It's their M. O. as TV cops say. Their mode of operation. First time in an actual bank robbery. Last time, too. As far as I'm concerned.

Why hadn't I read their minds? Or the thoughts of any of the customers who were inside and knew this was a robbery. Why hadn't I sensed any danger before we stepped into the damn bank? Why wasn't I getting a whiff of anything now? Even now?

A door opened and I turned my head toward the tellers in their walled cages. The three tellers were in a flurry of activity. The opened door showed the profile of a third well-dressed man, also wearing dark glasses. As he backed further out the door, I saw he held a long-barreled gun that reminded me of "The Rifleman"'s sawed off rifle. Modernized, certainly. It was aimed at the tellers behind the wall.

So. Each has his own distinct weapon of choice. But the robbers all look the same. I think I get it. No distinguishing features to describe to police. Each using a different oddly-shaped new-fangled weapon. Also hard to describe. Damn clever shit.

My face and jaw pressed against the cold floor, I was getting a crimp in my neck.

At least I know I still have vertebrae. Thought my spine had turned to jelly.

"Uncomfortable," I muttered.

Our guy, Robber One, knelt toward me and put his ceramic pistol close to my eye. "So is this if I use it," he said. "So keep your trap shut."

Not so courteous, after all. Still, the threat was made with a modicum of calm.

I shivered and felt the sharp tingling of pulses touch off the muscles of my arms and legs. *God, I hope he doesn't see me shaking. Can't control it.*

The second robber, the one with the nasty stick-insect weapon, began collecting cash from the customers on the floor around him. He stuffed the money in a canvas bag, the kind some business types carry when they plan to go to a sports club after work. I've seen that quite often. It's the current trend.

Out of the corner of my eye, I saw Robber Three at the door to the teller cages, marching the three tellers out. He made them drop to the floor. Robber Three also held a canvas sports bag that was bulging at the seams.

Robber Three nodded to our guy standing over us, Robber One. I didn't see Robber One's response. But –

Outdoors in a playground. By the swings. Our guy/Robber One was pushing a small boy on a swing. Definitely our guy, hair long and flowing in a strong breeze. He had a thick mustache and a short sprout of chin hair. He wore blue jeans and a long-sleeved pullover. Smiling broadly, he engaged in friendly repartee with the boy on the swing. I saw these things from Robber One's perspective.

He was thinking of that scene, longing to return to it. With my reception of the thought, I knew he was married, had a daughter as well as the son, and two short-haired terriers. His wife was blue-eyed and trim and blonde-haired, and very pretty. All those aspects of his life radiated from his mind.

I lifted my head off the floor to find his eyes. "You don't want to be here," I murmured softly.

"What was that?" Larry, flush on the floor next to me, whispered.

"Not you," I said tersely. I kept my eyes on Robber One. *You want to be with your wife. Your kids.*

Robber One looked at me. "Shut your trap." He rubbed his forehead as if in pain.

"You don't want to do this," I whispered.

He stared at me, his head nodding once, involuntarily. He murmured, "I don't want to do this."

Perspiration slid down the back of my neck. *I'm doing this! I'm actually doing this!*

"What's up with you?" asked Robber Two, rushing up to Robber One. He gestured to the door with his canvas bag. "Check outside. We're almost done here." As our guy went shakily to the door, Robber Two pointed at Larry and me with his stick-insect weapon. "Take out your wallets. Slowly."

This guy was a tough nut to crack. Loner. Unmarried. Didn't play well with others. Moved from town to town. No close friends. Images flowed from him of pretty young women sitting or lying in varying places, those images racing through his mind in rapid succession.

"Here." Larry lifted himself off the floor and tossed his wallet at Tough Nut. It struck him in the face.

"Stupid asshole!" swore Tough Nut, and he lifted his weapon, ready to smash the jutting barrel into Larry's face.

Larry grabbed the protruding rod-like end and struggled to pull the weapon away. Both Three and One ran toward us. Tough Nut twisted the weapon and threw Larry over backwards. Robber One was taking aim at Larry's back with his ceramic pistol.

I shouted something unintelligible and jumped to my knees, insane with fear for Larry. Something hot scalded the back of my calf.

Hot! Hot!

My eyes blurred as I stared at Robber One, his finger on the trigger of the ceramic gun directed at Larry. I found my focus:

That gun is hot! It burns. It burns.

Robber One screamed in pain and dropped the gun. Robber Two/Tough Nut turned to stare. Larry wrenched his stick-insect weapon out of his hands. At that same moment there was the sound of a crack followed by a whoosh coming from the area of the bank tellers and the third robber. My ears hurt from the sound.

Heat radiated down my arm and I turned to face Robber Three aiming his short rifle at me. The air at the end of its barrel seemed to shimmer. I was suddenly aware of weakness throughout my body and blood dripping down my coat sleeve. I sensed nothing from Robber Three as he stared back at me.

You feel weak. I did – so I made it HIS imperative. *You can't hold that weapon. So heavy. Tired. You want to sleep. That's all you want to do. Rest. Sleep.*

The rifle clanged against the floor.

Involuntarily, my legs collapsed and I slid in slow motion to the floor.

My last thoughts: *Not again. Not this soon. No more hospitals.*

CHAPTER THIRTY
So . . . What's Changed?

"Look at it this way," Larry said. "You're not hurt. At least not too badly. They said you'll be able to go home today. And this time you weren't killed. Are you going to finish eating that?"

Larry stood beside me as I lay on a gurney in a long corridor of the hospital emergency room, pointing at my tray of so-called food. He was eyeing the tuna sandwich that I had bitten into and left on the plate.

"Go ahead," I told him. "I don't feel like eating a thing."

I was propped up on the gurney, my left arm heavily bandaged and the back of my right calf covered with a large swath of gauze and tape. My arm throbbed terribly and sent shivers of pain from my shoulder to the fingers of my left hand. I looked at my fingers and watched them shake uncontrollably.

We were part of several long rows of patients on mobile beds and wheelchairs lining the walls. Men and women in medical garb strode quickly through the packed corridor, some stopping to check on patients before moving on.

Dr. Sanjay, the resident who had bandaged me half an hour before, came over. "Are you feeling much pain?"

"My arm feels like it's on fire. I can't stop the shaking."

"Got to tell you," he said, "I've never seen anything like this before."

"Like this? What do you mean? I thought I was shot. I saw the gun. Kind of a short-barreled rifle, like I've seen on TV."

"Well, what you were hit with were ice pellets. At least, that's what I found in your skin, largely turning into water, and then, gone. You were lucky; they could have penetrated deep enough to reach vital organs. They hadn't. But if any had, you might have died. Never saw anything like it before."

Larry asked, "So there weren't any bullets? Any real bullets?"

Sanjay looked at him and replied, "You are?"

"Mr. Brocton's friend. I'm an attorney." Larry started to reach into his jacket, then stopped himself – about to offer his business card? – "Lawrence Coates, Attorney At Law." I feared he would add "That's Coates with a silent 'e.'" But he didn't. "What kind of gun fires ice pellets?"

"I don't know. Never saw anything like this. But maybe, an air gun? Something specially made for the purpose? I just don't know."

I winced from the sudden increasing throbbing of my arm. "Damn! Why does it hurt so much?"

Sanjay took my arm and pressed the bandage. "I made this tight. That's what's doing it. I'll redress it before you go. You should be fine."

"When do you think I can go home?"

"I want to check your wounds again. Make sure there's no infection. I'll be back to do that in about --" He looked at his watch. "Twenty minutes. Hang tight."

Dr. Sanjay moved on. We saw him at the nurse's station conferring with other doctors. Then we lost track of him.

"So, what did you do?" Larry asked. "At the bank. To those robbers. Something was stopping them. And I was watching your face. Man, YOU stopped them. That WAS you, wasn't it? What did you do?"

"I'm more interested in how the police got in," I countered. "Who called them?"

"I think one of the tellers pushed a silent alarm. That's what I overheard from some of the conversation between the other customers, anyway. While the ambulance EMTs checked you out and the cops questioned us in the bank." He gave me one of his boyish, all-knowing grins. "So, tell me: what did you do? You were doing something more than reading their minds, right? What was it?"

That's right. I hadn't told Larry anything about my newly discovered ability to reach into people's heads and get them to respond. I was still shaken about having manipulated those robbers. Hell, I was scared out of my mind! This shaking — it was from knowing that I really could make people do things. Do you imagine it's easy to delve into people's minds? Do you think that's fun? No. Not on your life. I was shaking because I didn't know what I might see — and how I would be affected.

During the robbery, I acted out of need. Could I actually exert mental control over someone at will? Could I deliberately influence a person's mind? Someone like my friend Larry, for instance . . .

"Whoa! What was that?" He took a step back and held up his hands in a warding gesture. "You just did something, right? It felt like my scalp was itching. Like, man, I heard my name. It was as if you were calling to me but – inside my head. It's something new, isn't it? What is it?"

Do I tell him? Or put him off. This wasn't the best place to share such things after all. The middle of a crowded emergency room.

I looked around at the other patients and their visitors. They weren't paying any attention to Larry or me. And I wasn't reading anything from them. They were strangers. They were nothing to me.

I turned to Larry and held his eyes. "I can make suggestions," I said.

"Like what?" His face was blank but then he nodded. "Oh, like 'Drop that silly-looking pistol in your hand.' And the guy would do that. Is that it?"

"Something like that."

Larry tapped my shoulder. "Go ahead. Do me."

"What?"

"Suggest something in my mind. Come on."

"What am I supposed to suggest? I can't think of a thing."

"Something that's contrary to my nature. Something that's not like me at all."

"How do I know what's contrary to your nature?" But then it dawned on me. I had it! Grabbing his hand for emphasis, I closed my eyes and leaned toward him in what I supposed was "a proper mental state" as I exerted a thought. He winced.

His face showed confusion. He blinked several times, then stared pointedly at me. "So . . . what's changed?"

"What do you think of my sister?" I asked.

"Who? Your sister? Why bring her up?"

"I thought you had some feelings for her."

Larry tilted his head as if trying to remember. "Just a little brat. Always tagged along when we were kids that summer in Monticello. Why?"

"What's her name?"

"What?"

"What's my sister's name?"

"Come on, man! It's . . ." He tried to give it voice. Tried. Couldn't. "Well, you know. She's – Her name . . ."

"Do you like her?"

"No. Miserable little kid." He nodded, realizing that I did something to him. His face showed his puzzling it over. *What? What?* "Okay. I get it. You did something to me. Contrary to my nature. I know that much. So, tell me. What's changed?"

"Your taste in girls."

"But I like girls."

"What about my sister?"

"Miserable little brat." He stared at me and grinned. The line of his lips quivered with doubt. "What did you do? How am I changed? I'm still the same, aren't I? Come on, Alex!"

"I guess it didn't work on you."

He didn't see it. He couldn't put his finger on it. It was missing from his thoughts. That was all there was to it.

I DID THAT.

CHAPTER THIRTY-ONE
Back to the Grindstone

Nathaniel Sarker jogged through Bowen Park, crossing dirt paths and passing other joggers along the sidewalk as he reached the outer causeway. Finding a long stretch of path, he sprinted. Liam was with him.

In his soft rasping voice, Liam said, "How are you feeling?"

"As good as I'll ever be," Nathaniel answered.

Nathaniel pulled into a fast jog. Liam remained with him. Suddenly, Nathaniel felt a sharp pain at the back of his head. It broke his stride. He stopped and shook out the tightness, massaging his neck.

"Why the hell do you have to do that, Liam?"

"Something ahead. That car. I'm getting a bad feeling."

"Just because you get these feelings you've got to jump around in my skull?"

"I can't help it, Nathaniel. I'm wired that way. It's an autonomic reflex."

A dark green sedan slowed as it came toward him. It came to a stop.

Detective Matias stuck out his head. "How are you doing, Mr. Sarker?"

How should Sarker respond? He'd have to be suspicious. So what could he say?

Yes. I'm back to the grindstone. Getting back to my writing of the new novel, <u>Symbiote Sight</u>. You remember the premise, don't you? Liam is a microscopic extraterrestrial living inside Sarker's brain. Well, you'll see more of this as I work further.

My literary agent, the luscious Tracy Lessing, insisted that I finish the novel as soon as possible. I had been discharged from the hospital two nights ago and planet Tracy had been probing me to get it done. My bandages came off yesterday and I'm spending the weekend creating pages.

So, here I was, standing at my computer on Saturday morning, totally naked and plugging away:

"Problem," Liam rasped in his ear. "Those detectives are following you."

"So your instincts are good. What are you worried they'll find out?"

"They may find out about me."

Nathaniel stopped running. Leaning against a bench, he stretched his legs. "There is no you," he said. "There's nothing to find out. You don't really exist."

"I am surprised at you, Nathaniel. After all you know. You have seen me . . ."

"I've seen something in my eyes in the mirror. Something that looked back at me. But I could've imagined it. That doesn't mean you're real."

Nathaniel was suddenly conscious of other runners around him. He clamped his mouth closed. Two men jogged past, followed by a young woman in a sweat suit. She smiled briefly at him as she ran by. Nathaniel took up his jog, moving at a fast clip, and headed out of the park.

Even though he wasn't actually talking aloud, he felt more comfortable communicating with Liam on the less-trafficked sidewalks on his way home.

"Look," he began, his lips moving silently, "there isn't anything the police can find out, is there? You can't be detected, isn't that right?"

"Of course not. No instrument in your world can read me. But I also have no means of learning what other Kirii may be doing. There may be others observing us, perhaps one of those investigators. I don't like the one called Matias."

"You think he's inhabited by another Kirii?"

"Inhabited? That's a good way to put it, Nathaniel. I don't know if he is."

"You can't tell if there's a Kirii inside him?"

"No. I don't even know if other Kirii have ever communicated with a host body."

"What do you mean?"

"I've never done this before," Liam said. "Communicated with a human host."

Stronger.

Nearing the end of my novel.

Soon.

Five or six chapters to go, I estimate.

And as I write, as I clear page after page, chapter by chapter, I become stronger. It's deeply satisfying to see the conclusion just ahead, just beyond the discoveries that Sarker makes in my novel. Sarker is discovering more about the alien named Liam; discovering more about himself. I guess I do that also. Self-discovery is certainly there in the writer as he proceeds.

There. Something more. Coming to me now . . .

"Do you mean you've inhabited other people before me?"

"Of course. I've lived with five human hosts. You're the sixth."

"Five other people? And I'm the first one you've communicated with? Why me?"

"Because you keep putting yourself in danger."

"Five other people before me, you say. You must've been doing this for a couple of hundred years, then. Living silently inside them, observing. Did you care about them when you inhabited them? Did they matter to you?"

"Yes, Nathaniel. Every one of them."

"Then, what the hell do you want?"

"I haven't been given an assignment to take over your mind. There's no invasion force coming. I'm simply here."

"Why? What are you getting out of this? Conscious existence? Nothing more?"

"I feel a kinship with you, as I did with the others. I'm learning about you, each of you. My memories, my experiences, they come from those I inhabit. I've watched live vaudeville in New York, lived through the San Francisco earthquake, traveled by sailboat to Cuba before Fidel Castro took over. Joyous times. Dangerous times. Unforgettable times."

"What about your memories of your own kind? How did the Kirii get here?"

"I only remember bits and pieces. We drifted here, unaware. Species memory is like that – part instinct, part enlightenment."

"Okay. When I die – I will eventually, at a ripe old age – what happens to you?"

"It's an uplifting. Literally. I exit your body with your soul. For me, it's an esoteric experience."

"Wait. You're saying that you depart when the host dies. How then do you go on to another host?"

"There is always

"There's always THIS!" came planet Tracy's voice as I felt her breath at the hairs of my neck. She wrapped her arms around my shoulders and her naked legs converged about my thighs. We fell backwards to the plush carpet in my bedroom.

"What are you doing?" I yelled. "I was getting into the writing, Tracy. Come on!"

"You'll get back to it," she answered. "But first --"

She slipped from under me and straddled me as I lay on the carpet. Grasping my shoulders, she pressed her nude body against mine. Cool body. Soft supple body. Touching. Clenching. We delved deeply into each other's physical being. Her sensationally swelling body, alive and undulating. Her mouth covered mine, tongue searching, lips exploring, eyes soulfully flickering. She was everywhere at once. And I was part of her. I was her plaything. I was the soul she sought.

She was Nathaniel Sarker and I was her Liam.

CHAPTER THIRTY-TWO
What Did You Do to Larry?

"Funeral March of a Marionette" pierced the fragrant atmosphere of planet Tracy. My euphoria lifted and I was drifting between the rapture of Tracy's touch and the reality of lying on the carpet of my bedroom, the ominous music of Hitchcock's theme thrusting everything aside.

"Don't . . ." Tracy moaned as I shifted my weight from under her.

"I've got to check. It might be important."

My spine creaked as I dragged myself up from the carpet. I went to the desk to get my phone. Tracy moaned again, turned on her side, and drifted off once more, a world unto herself. I longed to rejoin her.

The ID on my phone showed it was Aly.

"Aly," I said, keeping my voice neutral. "How are you?"

"What the hell did you do to Larry?" came Aly's tension-edged rasp. When angry, she was never shrill. No hysterics. Simply harsh-toned and rasping.

Oh, Aly," I answered with all the jollity I could muster. I watched Tracy roll delicately on the carpet, grasping one of my favorite shirts in her arms. "Is there something wrong with Larry?"

"Don't you pull any shit on me. I know you too well. Either you did something to him or the two of you are pulling the most inane practical joke I've ever seen."

"What seems to be the matter?"

"You know. He can't say my name. He doesn't remember anything about me. Is this some stupid joke you two cooked up?"

"Sounds like he's becoming forgetful. What would I know about it?"

"I don't have time for this. Who's there with you? Wouldn't be your literary agent, would it? Tracy? She there?"

She got to me with that. It felt like she was reading my mind. She couldn't, but she had something like it – intuition, I guess. Always had. This wasn't funny any longer.

"Who's on the phone?" Tracy muttered from the floor, half asleep. "Someone say my name?"

I turned to her. She clamped onto my leg and sleepily tugged, nearly toppling me.

"Stop that," I grumbled. "It's my sister on the phone. Go back to sleep."

Tracy lay back and began snoring softly. *Did I do that?* "No, Tracy, just doze. Lightly. I'll get back to you in a minute."

Aly's voice came through again. "Everything all right there? That was Tracy, wasn't it?"

"Yes, I'm with Tracy. You're right. Okay, let me tell you. I got something extra after I was beaten by that fan in Philly."

Silence on the line.

"Aly?"

"Okay. Go on."

"Do you really want to know?"

"You can get into people's minds."

"I can get into people's minds. And I can suggest things."

"Did you just suggest that your girlfriend go to sleep?"

I looked over at Tracy. She breathed softly into my shirt. "Yes. I guess I did. But it wasn't intentional."

"Don't you ever try that with me. You hear me? NEVER."

"No. 'Course not." There was no playing with Aly.

"I mean it, Alex. And don't you dare tell anyone else about it. AND don't do it with anyone else. You could get into big trouble." Her tone had changed. She was my little sister and she was suddenly worried about me. I realized that without the need to see into her mind.

My hand began to shake as I held the phone. "To tell you the truth, I'm scared. I'm just discovering it for myself. I don't know what to do about it. Maybe we should talk. Want me to come over? Maybe we should get Dad on the phone. Both talk to him."

A garbled sound came from Aly's end. Then, "I called you about Dad." She choked on the last word.

"Dad?" I heard my heart thump loudly in my ears and I felt cold all over. "What's the matter with Dad?"

"Karen called me."

Karen? Who the hell was Karen?

"She's been living with Dad. Dad's -- He had a heart attack. A massive heart attack. He's in Dade County Hospital. Alex? Alex . . ."

"I'll be over to your place as soon as I can. We'll fly down together."

"Alex. . ." She barely got her words out. "He's going to die."

CHAPTER THIRTY-THREE
Still, Life

The thing in the hospital bed was nothing like my father.

It was covered with thick white sheets, a plastic tent billowing in and out around its head. Tubes and wires crisscrossed the entire trunk of the body. Machines surrounded the bed, continuous beeping and oscilloscope screens expressing signs of life.

Aly entered the partitioned room first, followed by her husband Brian, with me trailing them.

The room was small and very bright. The thing in the bed was dwarfed by the apparatus around it. When I came close to look at the thing, I stared down through the tent, feeling the in and out movement of the plastic, like the thing's final breaths, on my face. Tubes threaded into its mouth and tabs at its nose fed it oxygen.

All I could recognize were the eyes and the patch of flesh above them. Its eyes were closed but I knew them, and the eyebrows, and the creases that lined the forehead. Those things were human. Those things were familiar to me.

That much was Dad.

I so wanted it to be Dad. *Dad. Can you open your eyes? Please. Dad. Open your eyes.*

"He looks so small," Aly said.

"No!" I cried from out of a haze of fear and utter distress. "No! That's not Dad! He's not even here."

Brian grabbed me around my shoulder. "Easy. I know you're upset. So's Aly. But it's no good to fly off the handle."

Gazing at him, I felt an intense hatred. *Platitudes? Platitudes from an outsider? That does no good. That's nothing at all.*

"What was that?" he asked. "You think of me as an 'outsider?' Don't you dare! Not after these years of being with Aly! Not when I've been as close to your father as anybody. Closer than you these last few years! He's been 'Dad' to me but he's also let me call him 'Sam.' So don't you call me an outsider."

"I didn't say you were an outsider."

"I heard you."

"I didn't say it!"

"I heard you. It was your voice, damn it!

"Stop it!" shouted Aly. "You're arguing over nothing. When Daddy's . . ."

Brian embraced her. "Sorry, Aly. I went over the top. That wasn't like me." He went to me and put out his hand. "Sorry, Alex. Clearly, this is upsetting to all of us."

Fury and haze were slowly lifting as I stared into Bri's frank, ingenuous eyes. "Forget it. I said things . . ." I was ready to say '-- things I didn't mean,' but I didn't want to give out with platitudes of my own. Instead, I clamped shut.

"Wait a minute," Aly said, her eyes on the thing in the bed. She stepped to the side of the thing and bent close to the plastic tent. She straightened and looked from Brian to me. "What did you do to Bri?"

"I didn't do anything."

"What do you mean?" asked Brian. "What could he have done?"

Ignoring Brian, Aly stared fixedly at me. "You reached Bri's mind. Maybe you didn't intend to, but you did. What was it? 'Outsider?'" She turned to Brian: "Is that what you heard?"

"Yes. As clear as day."

She continued, "Anything else? How did it make you feel?"

"Angry." He looked at me. "I was so damn furious at you. I was ready to kill you. I have no idea why I felt that way."

"You did that," she said.

She had me perplexed until I thought about it.

"Well, maybe I did," I answered, uncertain even as I spoke. "I was angry. And hurt. But I wasn't trying to suggest anything to Brian."

"Suggest anything?" Brian said. "What's that supposed to mean?"

With a sweep of her hand that included me, Aly told him, "He reads minds. And something more, now. He can suggest things to people he can reach."

"Oh," he replied. "That explains it."

Aly and me: "Explains what?"

"At the chess game in the Village. It looked like you were signaling that female detective playing my friend Karl. You seemed to be communicating. I didn't see how you were doing it. Now, it makes sense."

"You do understand," I said, "that we're talking about mind reading. Something beyond the normal. You know, extrasensory perception."

"Of course."

"You're accepting it a tad more easily than I'd expect."

"That's the only way –"

Aly cut in: "Something more." She looked at me. "You were doing something more than making a suggestion. Something you're not aware of."

With an open-handed gesture, I asked, "What?"

She touched Brian's arm. "You say you were angry?"

"Very angry," Brian answered.

"And it was sudden? You weren't feeling that way when we walked in here?"

"No. Not at all."

"What are you saying?" I asked.

"You gave Bri that feeling. You transferred your own feelings to Bri."

"Okay. So what?"

"Dimwit! Don't you get it? You can transmit emotions to anyone else whose mind you can read. Who knows what else you might be able to do? You can even, I bet, create any kind of emotion in others that you want. You can make a happy person angry." Here she slapped Brian's arm. "And, presumably, make a hateful person feel glad about things. You might even bring an impaired person to alertness."

"I don't know that that's even possible. I don't know that I can do anything like that."

"You've got to try. You've got to do it with Dad. You can communicate with him, at least. Don't you think?"

"I don't know. Dr. Brawley told us he's in a coma. He may not come out of it. I don't know if I can look into Dad's mind. Aly, I'm scared. I don't think I want to try."

"This isn't the time to be scared! Nobody else can reach him. You may be able to wake Dad up. He may be able to talk to us. Isn't that worth a try?"

"What if Dad's already dead?"

She gestured at the machinery. "These show he's alive. There's the EKG. It's showing his brain is active."

"I don't know, Aly. I tried to read Dad when we came in. I got nothing."

"Try again!"

"What if he goes? I mean, what if he is dying, even now, and I go in. I don't know what I'll find. I don't know what will happen to me!"

"That's what you're afraid of?" Aly stared at me in a clear rage. "You haven't had that problem before. Not with all your readings of people. Why worry about such a thing now? There's nothing that's ever shown that anything will happen to you. Right?"

"That's exactly it. I don't know. This thing about touching someone's mind and altering it – that's all new to me. I'm too scared to try. I feel that someth –"

"Shit! That's Daddy in there! I want to talk to him. I need to talk to him!" She turned away from me and stared at the hospital bed. I sensed a quick alteration in her temperament. "Let's do it this way," she said, turning back to me. "Reach into *my* mind. Bring me

195

along when you try to read Dad. I'll be right there with you. You won't be alone."

"I don't know if that's possible! Besides, it doesn't matter how many –"

Her hands were around my throat. Thrust backward, we both fell against a heavy chair and tumbled to the floor. Aly didn't loosen her grasp around my shirt collar.

"GIVE DAD YOUR OWN THOUGHTS. If you can't find anything in his mind, give him YOUR memories! Give him YOUR emotions! Fill his mind! Get him to wake up! Do that!"

Dr. Brawley, the specialist in charge of my father's case, rushed through the curtain to Dad's compartment. He saw Aly and me on the floor and, as Brian helped Aly up, the doctor got me on my feet.

"I don't know what's going on between you two," Dr. Brawley said in a sharp voice. Wearing a white jacket, he was tall and slender, with thinning steel-gray hair, and a pencil–thin mustache. "But this has to stop. This is the coronary ICU. We can't --"

"Yes, Doctor." It was Brian who responded. "We're very sorry about this. Allow me to explain."

From my vantage, I couldn't tell if Brian had taken Dr. Brawley's arm or not, but Bri seemed to move the doctor bodily out of the compartment. I caught a glimpse of a smile on Brian's face before the two of them disappeared. I tried reading Bri's thoughts but all I caught was the numeral 7 dancing with a number 2 in his imagination. I had the distinct but unconfirmed impression that I was seven and Aly was two and I wondered why. I exited his mind feeling a bit of vertigo.

Aly glared at me in silence, her eyes red and fierce. I stood facing her, uncertain what to do or say. The ferocity of her argument – "Give Dad YOUR memories" – resounded off the walls of my mind.

"Okay," I said, not quite believing I was speaking the words. "Okay. But I want to take it one step at a time. I'll see if I can sense anything first. Then I'll try to pick up Dad's sensations – images of us or pieces of his own memories. After that I'll delve further. We'll see what happens. As for you . . ."

"What can I do to help?"

"Think about Dad. Keep your mind open. I don't know how far I can take this, but if I can really transfer thoughts, I may be able to use your memories of Dad to help me."

"So, what do I do?"

"Okay. Let me think. Show me Dad, as you'd like to remember him."

She directed a memory at me. Dad dressed in a tuxedo, bowtie in disarray – her wedding day. She saw him sitting beside her on a wood bench, taking her hand and speaking earnestly. Even if they hadn't had such a moment during the actual wedding day, she imagined it happening. Accompanied by pleasure and a sense of belonging.

I stood beside the thing on the hospital bed and leaned close to the plastic tent. I gazed at those closed human eyes and the unmoving creases of that forehead.

Dad? Dad? Open your eyes. Tell me how you feel. I need to hear your voice. Dad. Open your eyes. See me.

I entered the interior world that was not our reality. I had been there before. It was the landscape of my own dying, the few times I died or thought I had. Here I was again.

Only – this was different. I wasn't dying.

CHAPTER THIRTY-FOUR
My Mouth Full of Cobwebs

Fingers in the darkness, moving specks of dust, smearing particles of whiteness into dull shades of gray into deep purple into purple shot through with streaks of yellow.

The fingers daub at the rich purple, broadening the yellow spattering and adding blots of brown and green and stark gray patterns into the mix. Turning, turning, the digits of those fingers splash reds that become thick running juices layering the vast canvas. Taking position in the lower portion of the churning vista, the fingers become spackled stalks rising vertically into the dappled-sodden purple to blue to lavender sky.

A blaze of white!

Coalescing, gaining focus, the vertical stalks manifest into skyscrapers of sleek glass and glimmering steel. The Manhattan skyline at dawn: the Chrysler Building, the Empire State Building, and, downtown, the Twin Towers.

I never got to see the Twin Towers, I realized. *Not in real life. Nine-eleven was twenty-seven years ago.*

And I knew that this was not my vision of the world. These thoughts belonged to someone else.

Dad?

"Have you gotten to him? Alex! Are you talking to Dad?"

Aly nearly brought me out of my reverie but I held fast. Ignoring her, I saw the skyline fall back, and then I was viewing Manhattan through a frame cut in a wall, and pulling back farther, it became a familiar window. It was my parent's home in Whitestone, Queens. Mom, her back to me but form and wildness of hair instantly recognizable, was looking out the window. And then she turned to me. She was younger than I ever remembered her, her face smiling and so softly smooth. She reached out and took my hand and I came into view and it wasn't me, Alex, no. It was Dad. Young and tanned, wearing a black mustache, the ends lifting from his lip.

Dad never had a mustache!

The two of them embraced, then turned toward me. Me? I wasn't in the picture. Not for a little time yet. Somehow I knew the *when.* This was happening when they first married, when they first moved into their home in Whitestone. That view out that window was the same one I recalled as a boy, sans the Twin Towers.

"Are you talking to Dad?" Aly's voice intruded. I saw her for the briefest of moments, her hand on my shoulder, trying but failing to be a part of the vision before me.

"Let me talk to Dad."

I turned my head and saw her in our common reality, the hospital compartment in Dade County, Florida. "I haven't reached him yet. Need more time."

Returning to the realm of this thing's-on-the-bed interior mind, I saw an infant in a yellow dress running across the carpet in our home in Whitestone. "That's Aly. I remember her that young. Is that my memory? Or is it Dad's?" *Oh, God! I said that aloud!*

From a distance came Aly's voice, "Dad! Did you say my name? Alex, did he say my name? Daddy, I need to talk to you!"

As if in answer, I saw Dad – so young – chasing behind Aly, picking her up, and she laughed delightedly. She continued laughing as Dad slipped and fell, crying out in pain. Mom rushed over and they both stared at his bloodied toes while little Aly went on laughing.

I remembered seeing that when it happened but I didn't know anything further. Now I did. Dad had broken his foot. Ever since, he walked with a slight limp. I hadn't known why until he sent this memory.

This Memory! Dad! That's you! Wake up. I need to talk to you. Aly is here. She's standing right beside me.

Double-imaged, I saw his eyelids flutter, then his eyes squinted under the oxygen tent -- and I saw a face forming in that interior world. Dad's face. No. Mine. But when I was a boy. In my pre-teens, about twelve. I was mouthing something, whole paragraphs of words, flowing silently from my lips. Then, it was Dad, lying in bed, half-asleep, lips moving, speaking, speaking –

Ahhhh. Looowaaa.

His eyes heavily lidded, he tried to seek me out, mouthing the sounds. He couldn't get his mouth under his control. The sounds – they continued – but they weren't voiced. They were coming from Dad's *mind.*

Myowww! Caawwww!

What is it, Dad? What are you trying to say?

Eyes gazing up from the plastic around his head: *Mouuthhhh . . .*

I don't understand.

Mouth, dry . . . so dry . . .

Yes, Dad. Dry. I know what that feels like. My mouth was like that, too. When I had died and then came back.

Mouth full of cobwebs. Am I dead?

No, Dad. The doctor said you were in a coma. I brought you out now. Into some kind of conscious state.

His eyes opened then. Wide, under the tent around his face. He gazed at me and I thought I could see the edges of his lips curl up in a smile.

"Huumm. Ehhh," he murmured out loud. From his interior realm, I heard, *I think I see Aly just behind you.*

Aly keeps saying she needs to talk to you. She needs to.

Dad, much younger, sat on a bench in a hallway, wearing a tuxedo, the bowtie askew. Opposite him sat Aly. It was her wedding day. Dad and Aly talked, mouthing words unheard.

I know . . . came Dad's thought. *I know . . . what Aly wants.*

What? What does she want? Something from you? What?

"He's awake!" Aly cried out, pushing me aside as she leaned over the tent around Dad's face. "Do you hear me? Can you talk?" She looked at me. "Was he able to talk to you?"

"Not in words," I answered. I scanned the room. We were still alone with Dad. "He's having trouble forming words. Except that . . ."

"Except . . . what?"

"I'm able to hear his thoughts. Somehow, I can hear him in full sentences. That's never happened before."

Aly eyed me closely. Then, "This is part of your new ability. Don't you think?"

"I suppose. This connection with Dad is different from any other I've experienced. I'm still discovering things about it. Even now."

In my mind, I continued to see Dad in his tuxedo. He reached out with a beckoning arm and his image of me, younger, also in a tuxedo for Aly's wedding, stepped forward.

Aly is too distant from where I am, Dad sent. *You be the conduit. I'll answer her through you. Go on. Let her ask what she wants. You can tell her my answers.*

"Dad will answer you," I told her. "Ask what you want."

She let out a sob and leaned closer to the bed. I felt the tension in her.

"Should I go to Philadelphia?"

I stuttered, "Why would you --?"

"Just ask!"

Aly wants to know if she should go to Philly.

I don't have all the answers. Tell her that.

What's that all about, Dad?

"What did Dad say?"

"He doesn't have all the answers.'

"Should I go see James?"

"James? *She means Jaime? My Jaime? Mr. Quiver?* "Why?"

"Just ask Dad."

I heard her, Son. Tell her: no. It wouldn't do James any good.

What's going on? I asked. *What do you know about Jaime?*

"What does Dad say?"

"He says you shouldn't go. It wouldn't do any good for Jaime."

"I can't sleep. I can't get any work done. Everything makes me nervous. I've got to tell someone. I can't keep it to myself any longer."

"What the hell are you talking about?" I asked.

Shut up, Alex! Don't pursue this now. Your sister is upset.

Why is she upset?

And then he showed me. I envisioned a younger version of Jaime – in his teens, before I became reacquainted with him. Black hair growing long, single brow across beady, wide-apart eyes, a crooked grin that was broader than I had ever seen. Then he turned away from me, looked towards a bedroom door behind him. I – or the viewpoint 'I'—moved to the door as it opened. Sitting up in the bed, under the covers, was Jaime's father – the resemblance and my comprehension of what I was seeing – was obvious to me—and next to him, naked under the blanket, was Mom. Mom Mom Mom.

. Dad confirmed what I suspected: *James Everett, son of my college friend William Everett, is your half-brother.*

"I've got to talk about it!" Aly shouted, then covered her mouth. She grabbed my sleeve. Softer, she said, "I've got to tell somebody. Dad understands. But you. I need to tell it. Alex!" Her voice had become shrill. Unnatural for my little sister, for my tough, steady, little Aly. "Alex! Let me tell you!"

"I'm listening."

"I was in the hotel room," she whispered.

"What hotel room?"

"Where that crazy fan was beating you up. I was hiding in the bathroom. I did it!"

"What?"

"I stabbed him. What was his name? Dennis something? I killed him!"

CHAPTER THIRTY-FIVE
I Held On

The woman's bloody sleeve with a green clover-shaped button.

I recalled that image myself, instantaneously. That was the piece of evidence Detective Ambrose revealed to me when I was in the hospital in Philly. Proof that Mr. Quiver had the help of a woman. Or Mr. Quiver *was* a woman. Or there was a conspiracy of several people that included a female.

"You were there?" I murmured. I remembered seeing a shadow moving through the open bathroom door in Dennis Leibowitz' room. "How could you have gotten into his room?"

"Housekeeping," Aly said. "The ladies who clean the rooms aren't security conscious. All I had to say was I was the wife and had to get back in my room for something. No problem."

"The Philly cops told me Dennis was killed with his own knife. How did you get it?"

I came out of hiding when that monster started slamming you in the head. I jumped on him and put him in a choke hold. He went for something in his pants pocket. First rule of my defensive training class: Don't wait until your attacker brings out a weapon."

"So, how did you get it away from him?"

"I poked him in his eyes. Hard. He screamed, grabbed me by the throat to push me away, and fumbled to hold his knife for a strike. I got hold of it before he could."

"Where was Jaime when that was happening?"

"Still locked out of the room. I let him in and he dragged that nut onto the bed."

"So you were actively working with Jaime?"

Wild Bill Everett. The thought came from Dad, articulated, his voice clear to me. *My old friend. We went to college together. I met Ruthie through him.*

Jaime's father. William 'Wild Bill' Everett, dressed in blue jeans and a sports jacket. Youthful and tough, dark far-apart eyes beneath black eyebrows, tall and muscular, a wry smile, lips open, seeming to make a coarse remark.

He had been going out with Ruthie for a year or so, Dad sent. *Then he introduced me to her. We both loved her.*

I found myself staring at Aly's tense face. I couldn't read her. "You met me before Dennis led me to his room. How much of that had you and Jaime planned?"

"You saw me drive away, sure." Aly said. "But I came back to the hotel after driving a few blocks. Jaime and I were both there, keeping an eye on you. When Jaime spotted that guy at the convention, he was on alert and called me back as I headed away."

I wished I could have seen my sister as a dewy-eyed fresh-faced innocent. But I stood there gazing at her and saw only that her mouth was grim, eyes hard and swollen, her voice gruff and hard-edged.

"Jaime shouldn't go to prison," she spewed out. "Not for that. He didn't kill anybody. It was me."

"Why were you there?" I asked, trying to shake myself out of the shock. "Why were you there at all? Watching me? Watching Dennis?"

Dad: *We've been watching you for a long time.*

"You've been watching me? Dad? You've been watching?"

"Dad?" cried out Aly. "Dad, I've got to go to Philadelphia. I can't let Jaime take the blame."

Jaime was born when Ruth was still in college. Wild Bill had graduated the year before. He took responsibility for the baby, even though they weren't married.

How could you have been watching me, Dad? You've been in Miami for more than four years now.

Modern technology, Son. Jaime and Aly kept me informed. You know. The telephone. The internet. Learned to use both a long time ago.

Was Mom part of it, too?

No. She never really understood what you could do. Remember that day when you were in the doldrums over losing your girlfriend? The day I took you with me on my bakery deliveries?

Of course. That's when you let me know that you realized what I could do.

Yes, of course I remembered. It was a revelation to me. Then and now, this minute. Then: Dad revealed he suspected I could read minds. He had practiced hiding his thoughts from me numerous times and, that day when I helped him with his deliveries, he let me see his thoughts quite deliberately. I was a teenager then. And he introduced me to Daphne, a woman he had loved in college BEFORE knowing Mom. Yes, a revelation: A man could be in love with more than one woman. And still be true. Now: This new revelation. Dad knew Mom's lover, the man she continued to see even after Dad married her. And HE knew. Dad was true to my mother AND his best friend. And Wild Bill stayed true to both of them also.

Aly looked at me and took my sleeve. "Did you tell Dad? What did he say?"

"No, I didn't ask him." I stared at Aly, wondering, *Why you? Why you and not me?* "You knew who Jaime was? All this time, you knew?"

Let me understand this, I turned to Dad. We sat on that bench in the reception hall of Aly's wedding, both in tuxedos. *You're Mr. Quiver? And so was Aly? And Jaime? Anyone else?*

Just us. Oh, Wild Bill stood by us, of course. But he died young. When James was a teenager, I think. Wild Bill hadn't turned fifty when his heart gave out.

Sending the thought to Dad but saying it aloud as well: "Why were you watching me all those years, without telling me anything?"

In the hospital room, distantly, Aly answered, "We knew you were special."

James so regretted strangling you when you were a child, Dad sent. *Wild Bill came to me with his son's worries over you years later. Around the time we opened that snack shop in Monticello that unique summer. After you were nearly blinded by that killer in our shop, I became very watchful of you. I started it. I put James and Alyson up to keeping tabs on you when they could. But I started it. I was Mr. Quiver.*

I was suddenly gripped in a heat of fury. Not at Dad but . . . I glared at Aly in our reality again. "Why were you let in on all this?

Why wasn't I a part of it?" My voice rose harsh and full of hate, more than I intended. "Why was I kept in the dark, Aly?"

Ohhhhh! came from Dad.

What's wrong? I asked.

Momentary twinge. My body reminding me I'm still here.

"You weren't the only one I was protecting," she said. "Remember? I told you at the convention that Mom needed to tell things to someone. She talked to me. Don't you realize?" She stopped and tears came to her eyes.

"Realize what?"

"I had to keep quiet about you. Mom didn't know anything about your ability. We all agreed it would be best not to tell her. She wasn't the sort –"

"What? What sort?"

"To believe that you could read minds. She wouldn't accept that. Dad saw the possibility by observing you but she never saw it."

I hated my sister! I wanted to grab Aly by the throat and strangle her.

"That's no reason to keep things from me! Damn you!"

I lunged. She fell back and I missed her neck, grappling with her and clasping her shoulders.

She shrugged me off and slapped my face. Hard. "Don't do that ever again!"

"Why couldn't you tell ME? Why did you leave me out?"

The EKG machine came alive with rapid bleeping. I looked down at Dad's body. His chest was heaving greatly. It became a double image, seeing Dad on the bench in his tuxedo clutching his chest while at the same time watching the rise and fall of his heavy breathing in our reality.

"Dad!" said Aly, staring horrified at the body on the hospital bed. "He needs help!"

"Wait," I said. "Dad?"

No, Son, Dad's inner voice rang out. *Alex. It was my decision. I made the choice. Aly had no say in the matter.*

Why? I sent. Dad and I were back in the hall, wearing our tuxedos, facing each other on the bench. *Why didn't you want me to know about Jaime and his father?*

His breathing eased. The bleeping of the machine slowed. Dad was calm again.

Because you were so rash. The way you put yourself in danger when you followed that killer in our shop. I recalled how you talked openly, when there were other people around us, about how you knew what he was going to do. You took chances. I didn't trust you.

What do you mean? Didn't trust me to do what?

Didn't trust you to keep quiet. I was working six days a week. I needed eyes on you. I needed Aly's eyes and James' eyes. We all kept track of you. You were bound to tell the wrong people what you could do. I was afraid. Afraid you would make mistakes. You've made that kind of mistake just recently. Do you even realize that?

What mistake?

Your friend. Larry Coates. Look what you did to him. Careless of you. Thoughtless of you actually. You can't change that so simply. Oooo —

What's wrong?

This is bad. Discomfort. Worse than --

All Hell swept away sight and sound and thought. The EKG started bleeping again, this time accompanied by the blasting of an alarm and the flashing of a red light. On the bed, the body that was my dad leapt up and collapsed.

Doctors and nurses rushed in. Dr. Brawley and Brian were right behind them. Brawley began giving orders. He joined the other doctors as they pushed the tent aside and detached tubes and moved equipment out of the way. Aly and I were shoved aside as they worked on their patient. Brian came over to Aly and held her tightly.

I couldn't find the reception hall or the bench or Dad. *Dad, Dad! Come back to me. I need you. We're not finished here.*

I don't want to leave you, Dad sent. *Not in control here. Pain. I can't . . . Reach for me. Hold on. Hold on. . .*

That's what I did.

I held on.

And I held on, too.

CHAPTER THIRTY-SIX
Creating Worlds

The funeral was on Monday, December 18th.

Aly gave the eulogy. It was poignant and humorous and had us all crying at the conclusion. Brian was there, of course, and Larry Coates, behaving unusually solemn. I caught him taking curious looks at Aly every so often. I feared (almost) that they would become friends again. Three of Dad's old friends were there. Cousin Howard from Metuchen, New Jersey also. And the two of us. That was it. Just we few.

It was drizzling out at the Long Island cemetery and we stood in muddy dirt as the pine coffin was lowered into the freshly dug trench. Gloomy, all in all, and quite appropriate for the occasion

Our small band of mourners gathered afterward at an Italian restaurant in Queens. Aly told me in a private moment that she decided to go to Philadelphia. She intended to speak to Jaime and abide by his wishes before taking any other action. It felt odd to hear her talk about a half-brother I barely knew. She carried a devotion for him in her voice and manner that made me feel terribly uncomfortable. Until then, I expected such a rapport to exist only between her and me.

I was so proud of her. She reminded me so much of Ruthie. I wish we could've told her the truth. But I don't know what the truth is. Do you?

No. There isn't any guidebook. No doctors I can ask for advice. I suppose it was that you weren't dead when I initially connected with you. You were in a coma, according to Dr. Brawley. What was that like for you?

Hard to say. I never had your imagination to work with before. Now . . . It was like being trapped in a closed box, sealed up. I don't know why a box. It was a box without limits. Timeless. Confining AND boundless. I felt I should be someplace but it wasn't defined by any useful dimensions. Doesn't make much sense, does it?

None of this makes much sense. In the usual sense.

When I heard your voice talking to me, I began seeing images of you at Alyson's wedding. I don't know why.

I asked her to picture you before I sought your mind. Perhaps it was my influence over you, or you picked up on Aly's thoughts through my connection.

Confusing. We're just guessing here aren't we? Am I dead? Or am I merely a figment of your imagination? That would really be strange. I don't feel imaginary.

I wouldn't like to believe that either. If that were so, that means I'm hallucinating, and perhaps even insane. I've looked in the mirror in my bathroom when I shave. My eyebrows are gray when they never were before. My eyes sit deeper in my face, the way yours did.

My eyes are blue. Yours are brown.

I know. But there are a thousand little things I see in myself that seem changed, that remind me of you.

When I asked you to hold on to me, what did you hold onto?

I don't know. I had lost the image of you at Aly's wedding. Let me think. It was like I was trying to grab hold of an oversized beach ball, so large that I couldn't get my arms around it. I felt static electricity flow through my hands. It felt sticky. I exerted energies from deep in my belly. I knew I was keeping you with me psychically but that was more intuitive than anything of substance.

So, where am I? Where do I reside?

You're here. We're both right here. I'm not dominating anything, and neither are you. We're a unique blend. We're sharing consciousness equally.

Consciousness. That's how it feels to me, too. But does that mean I am dead? What part of me is actually, physically here? My soul?

Like you had said, I don't have all the answers.

Well, I have questions. Lots of them. Like, what's going to happen to us now? You're the science fiction writer. Any thoughts?

My thinking is that over time we'll become one. Whatever this is of you – your soul or consciousness – will become part of me. My guess is, eventually, we won't think of one another. We will have become one entity.

You sound so sure of that, Son. Why are you, when I'm not?

I think it's the nature of what I write. In dealing with ideas in science fiction, I think on a cosmic scale – the Big Questions.

I can't accept that I'll simply fade away from this merging with you. Disappear? And go – where? Will I one day face an Afterlife? Will I somehow be joined with God?

I can't answer any of that for myself. We've both been so close to death. I suppose, for my part, I've been avoiding any deep thoughts about those things.

I had a thought. I know why I'm here.

Well, I told you. I held onto you before you actually died.

No. I mean the reason. The reason that goes beyond you and me.

You have me at a loss.

Of course I do. You wouldn't know. Why would you? It's the same reason I wanted you watched all those years when you were discovering your telepathic ability. You don't know what it has come to, do you?

No, I don't. I'm still discovering the extent of it.

But you will continue to explore it. You'll delve into your friend's – Larry Coates' – mind, won't you? You'll continue looking into people's thoughts. How can you not? You'll continue making suggestions that can alter the minds of others. You don't know what kind of damage you can cause. That's dangerous. You're dangerous.

I don't plan on doing anything to harm others. Aly warned me about making suggestions in anyone's mind. It scares me, Dad. I won't do it.

That's good. I've been afraid for you. Afraid you wouldn't know when to stop. That's why I'm here.

What are you going to do to help me?

You have to trust my powers of observation. Can you? Will you listen to me, even if I advise you to do something against your wishes?

Yes, Dad. Of course I'll listen. This is all new to me.

This is all new to everybody.

Well, if that's settled, I've got to get back to my usual routine. I try to put in a couple of thousand words every day. I'm eager to start the new novel.

Okay, Alex. How do I fit in with that? Am I going to be taking part somehow?

Of course.

What can I bring to your writing that you haven't had before? My experience is certainly different from yours. What does that add to your fiction?

A different perspective. Perhaps a sensitivity about people that I haven't had.

A sense of humor.

Dad! My novels are very humorous in spots. I have a great sense of humor.

I can bring a solemnity to your humor. Sardonic. Dark.

Dark? You? I hadn't seen that side of you.

You really know very little about me, Alex. So much of my feelings, my experience, my understanding of life, has been withheld from you.

I can see that this is going to be quite a learning experience.

For both of us. It will be quite a challenge for me to discover you, too. My son, the writer. So let's start. Show me what you have in mind.

World Shaper

By

Alex Brocton

Good title. But why 'World Shaper?' Where does that come from?

I want to explore the kind of mental telepathy that I have but fictionalize it. I'm interested in the expansion of the mind through near-death experiences. My protagonist will be somebody like me. He discovers that he has a developing telepathic capacity caused by a series of accidents. He exists in a world that is new to him. Potentially, he can reshape the thoughts of others, and in that way, change the world.

So you intend using your own experience to write about this young man.

Yes. As he discovers his abilities, he finds that he is being watched. Who is it? What does this mysterious observer want? As my protagonist seeks out those answers, he gains a wider perspective on his society and his place in it.

I can see how I can help you. While you pursue the extrasensory aspects of your novel, I can suggest details of your life that lend themselves to telling the protagonist's story.

Very good. Here's what I have in mind . . .

Alex and I returned to writing the novel. I sat at the keyboard and let him run the words across the screen. We worked as one. Hell! We were one.

Chapter One: Targeted

I was being watched. I'd been watched for years. He hadn't done anything to me and I'd never actually spotted him following me. But it was the same person whenever I caught him at it.

How did I know?

Because I recognized what he was seeing. Me. Oh, not as I am now at twenty-eight years old. No. Most often, what he envisioned was myself as a teenager with longish brown hair falling over my forehead.

Always that vision in his head. Some time ago, I figured out why. Whenever he decided he was close enough, he deliberately thought of that image of me. Only one reason why he'd do that.

He knew I could read his mind.